Bibliotheca Iranica
Persian Fiction in Translation Series
Number 4

In A Voice
Of Their Own

A Collection Of Stories By Iranian Women
Written Since The Revolution Of 1979

Compiled And Translated,
With An Introduction By

Franklin Lewis
and
Farzin Yazdanfar

Mazda Publishers
Costa Mesa, California
1996

Mazda Publishers
Since 1980
P.O. Box 2603
Costa Mesa, California 92626 U.S.A.
Web site: http://www.mazdapub.com

Library of Congress Cataloging-in-Publication Data

In a Voice of their Own: A Collection of Stories by Iranian Women
Written Since the Revolution of 1979/ Compiled and translated,
with an introduction by Franklin Lewis and Farzin Yazdanfar.
P. cm.—(Bibliotheca Iranica. Persian Fiction in Translation
Series, no. 4). Includes bibliographies

ISBN:1-56859-045-8 (alk. paper)

1. Short stories, Persian—Women authors—Translations into
English. 2. Persian fiction—20th century—Translation into English.
3. Women—Iran—Social conditions—Fiction.
I. Lewis, Franklin, 1961-. II. Yazdanfar, Farzin. III. Series.
PK6449.E7I6 1996
891'.5533080355—dc21   96-39171
CIP

انتشارات مزدا

In A Voice Of Their Own

Bibliotheca Iranica
Persian Fiction in Translation Series

Number 1
Sadeq Chubak
The Patient Stone
(0-939214-62-8, 1989)

Number 2
Goli Taraqqi
Winter Sleep
(0-9399214-42-3, 1994)

Number 3
Ja`far Modares Sadeghi
The Marsh
[Gavkhuni]
(1-56859-044-X, 1996)

For
Foruzan, Sahar and Ava -- FL
and
Farnaz and Paniz -- FY

Contents

Introduction

Iranian Women, the Short Story and the Revolution of 1979

Traditionally excluded from the public sphere, Iranian women discovered a legitimate outlet for their creativity in storytelling. From generation to generation, women handed down stories, poems, rhymes, and so forth, by word of mouth, and by this means gave voice to their life experience. This form of storytelling was not, however, accorded the status of literature, and was rarely written down; like Shahrazad (Scheherazade) in *One Thousand and One Nights (the Arabian Nights)*, women typically told their stories to small and private audiences. We do, of course, encounter some notable exceptions to this general rule, such as the poetesses Râbe`eh Qozdâri (10th century), Mahsati (11th or 12th century),[1] Zib al-Nesâ Makhfi (daughter of the Moghul emperor Aurangzeb, 1638-1701),[2] and Tâhereh (Qorrat al-`Ayn, 1814-1852).[3] Indeed, Parvin E`tesâmi (1907-1941),[4] Forugh Farrokhzâd (1935-67),[5] and Simin Dâneshvar (1921-), all women, would be included in any list of the most prominent Iranian literary figures of the twentieth century.[6] However, the number of women writers, or at least the number welcomed into the literary canon, is quite small considering the rich, thousand-year history of Persian literature.[7]

As writers of non-fiction prose, Iranian women began to appear in print in the late 19th century, primarily in advocacy of women's issues. One finds, for example, Bibi Khânom Astarâbâdi's *The Vices of Men (Ma`âyeb al-rejâl*, 1894), a plea for greater understanding of the lot of women in the patriarchal society of Iran and an indictment of the exploitative behavior of men, written in refutation of a treatise called *The Training of Women* (*Ta'dib al-nesvân*, a how-to manual for men to inculcate a submissive attitude in their wives and instill in them "proper behavior").[8] Such writings on the "woman's question," perhaps under the influence of the British, had emerged in print a generation earlier in India, where we find Nazir Ahmad (1830-1912) utilizing an example of two sisters, one good and the other bad, to illustrate the qualities of the successful and virtuous woman in his Urdu prose work, *A Mirror For Brides* (*Mer'ât al-`arus*, 1868).[9] The thrust of such arguments was often religious--an educated woman will be better able to observe religious law, to morally train and educate her children, and to run an efficient household.[10] We find a similar literary device, this time in the form of speeches by an imaginary Indian prince addressed to an imaginary Iranian prince, in Mirzâ Âqâ Khân Kermâni's *One Hundred Homilies* (*Sad khetâbeh*), a critique of the conditions prevailing in Iran. Kermani's work, written sometime prior to his death in 1896, apparently opens the discourse on the "woman question" in Persian.[11] By religion a Babi, Kermani was familiar both with the teachings of Sayyed `Ali Mohammad Bâb (1819-1850) about the status of women, and with the history of one of the Bâb's most prominent disciples, Qorrat al-`Ayn Tâhereh, who publicly unveiled at a conference of Babi leaders in Iran in 1848.[12]

The emergence of the public debate on the woman question in Iran therefore pre-dates the publication in Arabic of *The Emancipation of Women* (*Tahrîr al-mar'ah*, 1899) and *The New Woman* (*al-Mar'ah al-jadîdah*, 1901), by the Egyptian Kurd, Qâsim Amîn (1863-1908), though it was the publication of Amin's first book (translated into Persian the year after its appearance in Arabic by E`tesâm al-Molk, father of the above mentioned Parvin E`tesâmi), which initiated a lengthy and heated public debate on women's rights in the Muslim World.[13] During the Iranian Constitutional Revolution (1906-11), many polemical treatises, essays and satirical vignettes, often in verse, advocating improvement of the status and condition of Iranian women appeared in a variety of newspapers and journals, most notably in Sayyed Ashraf al-Din Gilâni's *The Breeze of the North* (*Nasim-e shemâl*, published in Rasht, 1907-1911?).[14] Women, who played an active and often militant role in the political events of the Constitutional Movement,[15] also entered the public discourse on the "woman question;" by 1910, *Knowledge* (*Dânesh*), a journal written for and mostly by women under the editorship of Dr. Kahhâl, began publication in Tehran. In addition to articles on the status and condition of women, health, hygiene, childcare, and recent medical and scientific discoveries in Europe, a significant portion of this journal was devoted to the serial publication of translations (rather literal) of stories from European languages, mostly English.[16] Eventually, these themes began to echo in literary works by Iranians.[17]

The reformist discourse on the condition and status of women resulted in a theoretical commitment to the education of women and led, in part, to the establishment of girls' schools in Iran, at first mostly private. Eventually, the government worked to expand compulsory primary education by providing public schools. The earliest Iranian women to receive a university education did so abroad; Ghodsieh Ashraf Khânum, for example, after studying in the American Presbyterian school in Tehran, travelled to the U.S. in 1911 and attended the Lewis Institute in Chicago, a junior college, from where she subsequently went on to Columbia University.[18] In 1938 the first women inside Iran, a group of twelve, were admitted to the University of Tehran, which had itself been founded three years prior.[19]

Meanwhile, Rezâ Shâh Pahlavi (r. 1921-41), who assumed the role of monarch after the downfall of the Qajar dynasty, consciously attempted to modernize and westernize Iran, emulating Ataturk's efforts in Turkey. On 7 January 1936 Reza Shah promulgated a law requiring that all women appearing in public in the cities of Iran must do so without their traditional veils. Iranian citizens of both sexes were also required to wear western-style clothing. Although many educated and upper-class Iranians welcomed the forcible unveiling, the Muslim clergy, as well as many women, felt that going out veilless was a sinful disgrace; some women remained at home for the entire five-year period this law was in effect rather than venture out incompletely attired. When the Allied powers overthrew Reza Shah in 1941, the wearing of a veil in public became optional.

From the 1940s, the Iranian communist party (Tudeh) began lobbying the parliament to grant women the right to vote and to improve women's legal standing within the family.[20] Several women's organizations also lobbied for the extension of the franchise to women. Under Mohammad Rezâ Shâh Pahlavi (r. 1941-79), the state granted women the right to vote in 1963 and strengthened their social standing with the passage of two Family Protection Laws in 1967 and 1975. These laws required a husband to obtain permission from his first wife before marrying a second (unless the first wife was mentally or physically unable to fulfill her family and matrimonial duties), effectively limiting, though not outlawing, polygamy. The Family Protection Laws also made court approval mandatory before a man could divorce his wife and granted women the right to petition the court for a divorce under certain circumstances. Though the passage of such legislation did not bring about equality of the sexes, the Iranian women's movement heralded these laws as a great victory.

After the revolution of 1979, the government of the Islamic Republic of Iran repealed many of the legislative and social changes of the Pahlavi era that were seen to conflict with the laws of Islam. Though Ayatollah Khomeini had opposed the extension of the franchise to women in 1963, women retain the right to vote today in the Islamic Republic of Iran. The Family Protection Laws, however, were suspended, thereby legally and socially re-enforcing polygyny; in theory, a man may have up to four permanent wives and an unlimited number of temporary wives (Article 942 of the Iranian Civil Code). Following Shiite law, the Islamic Republic permits a man to take on "temporary wives" (*Sigheh*) for a period of time pre-determined in a contract (Article 1075 of the Civil Code);[21] in 1990 this practice was officially encouraged as a means of addressing the problems of war widows and the sexual drives of young unmarried Iranians.[22] The laws of the Islamic Republic restrict a woman from traveling abroad without the permission of her husband. Though women can and do serve as members of parliament, the law does not permit them to function as judges, lawyers or jury-members. Among the possible penalties for prostitution and adultery are lashing or stoning. Despite a huge public protest in Tehran, in 1979 the veil was made compulsory for women outside the home. Those women perceived to be wearing too much make-up or not properly covering their hair and body in public have been periodically arrested, fired from their jobs, or otherwise threatened in the streets of Tehran. Co-educational schooling has been abolished.[23]

Western readers should not imagine, however, that all Iranian women feel powerless within their society or have been unable to articulate feminist concerns since the establishment of the Islamic Republic. Indeed, it has been argued that:

> ...in spite of the reversal for women under Khomeini's regime, the whole question of women's rights and social position has gained a prominence, unprecedented in ... Iranian history.[24]

One of the reactions to the interference in and domination of Iran by western powers, has been a rejection of the western bourgeois concept of women's liberation, which, it is argued, has intensified the sexual objectification of women in the west and broken down moral codes. An alternate Islamic view of women's liberation has been expounded by the western-trained sociologist, `Ali Shari`ati, in a series of lectures delivered in 1971, *Fâtemeh is Fâtemeh*, which argue that women must play an active role, separate from but equal to that of men, in the revolutionary transformation of society.[25] The young Iranian women of today, following the model set by Fatemeh, the daughter of the Prophet Muhammad, must be neither like traditional women, nor like the media-purveyed image of western women, but must become modernized, engaged Muslim women. Among the clergy, Ayatollah Motahhari, who was assassinated shortly after the Revolution, also denounced the western view of the liberated woman, insisting instead on protecting women by preventing the public fetishization of the female body; in his view, this entails veiling and the elaboration of a set of Islamic women's rights.[26]

Women and Persian Prose Literature

The image of women revealed in medieval Persian literature generally reflects the values of a patriarchal society, as one would expect. Ferdowsi, in describing the virtues of the wife of Anushirvân, the famous Sasanian king, stresses the qualities desirable in a woman:[27]

> *agar pârsâ bâshad o rây-zan*
> *yaki ganj bâshad parâkandah zan*
> *be-vizhah ke bâshad be-bâlâ boland*
> *foruheshtah tâ pây moshkin kamand*
> *xeradmand o bâ dânesh o rây o sharm*
> *soxon goftan-ash xub o âvây narm*

> If she be chaste and thoughtful
> a woman is a treasure bestowed,
> especially if she be tall of stature
> musky curls hanging to her feet;
> wise, knowledgeable, decisive, modest,
> her speech good and voice soft.

While this passage may reflect a particularly male-centered conception of female virtues, it at least ascribes virtues to women. By contrast, one frequently encounters blatantly misogynistic statements or attitudes on the part of the poets and mystics of the medieval period, who inherited a Hellenistic cultural prejudice toward women as intellectually inferior beings, and the neo-Platonic and monastic view of relationships with women as ties that bind men to the world and prevent them from pursuing heroic labors of strength or spirit. Nevertheless, in the romances of this period, we often encounter noble and self-possessed women, whose behavior acts as a silent reproach to the men around them. Nezâmi (d. 1191), for example, speaks highly both of his mother and of his wife, who provided the model for his character Shirin, a powerful, independent woman, in control of her own sexuality.[28]

It should be noted, however, that women, even heroines with strong personalities of their own, rarely play a leading role or stand on their own; rather, they are almost always defined in relationship to a male character. This is true of most genres of Persian literature, and should be understood as representative of traditional Persian culture in general. As Erika Friedl notes of the Persian folktale:

> With very few exceptions, then, women, no matter where they actually stand in the plot, are defined primarily in terms of their significance to one or several men, while men are never discussed in terms of their significances to women....Women develop a certain character of their own only when they are "alone," that is, without a father, brother or husband.[29]

Whereas Iranian women have played supporting roles in literature, in real life, the verbal skills of Iranian village women (in the estimation of at least one anthropologist), ironically outshine those of their male relatives:

> Women were more verbally gifted and active than men. Spending more time than men in the company of family, relatives, and neighbors with whom they felt comfortable and natural, less compelled by dignity to restrict themselves to "important" topics of conversation, less restrained from undignified probing and pressuring, and known to be more curious and gossipy, many women developed amazing communication and information collecting skills....Women used their verbal and intellectual skills for gathering information, spying, persuading, taunting, berating, threatening, shaming, discussing, interpreting, encouraging, and building up close sociopolitical relations.[30]

Such uses of linguistic talent, however, were not generally accorded status as literature, and if a woman did compete within the arena of the accepted literate genres, her efforts were often viewed as curiosities or marvels, rather than primarily as works with their own intrinsic aesthetic value. Occasionally, however, literary sources allude to the power that a woman might wield by virtue of her verbal gifts, such as Shahrazad, in *the Arabian Nights* cycle, who was able to stay the executioner's hand, reform her husband--the king's--behavior and eventually establish justice throughout the kingdom through her cleverness, goodness, and her stories.

In tracing the development of modern Persian literature, critics often consider *The Travel Diary of Ebrâhim Beyg* by Zayn al-`Âbedin Marâgheh'i (published in three volumes during the first decade of the 20th century) or Mirzâ Habib-e Esfahâni's Persian adaptation of James Morier's *The Adventures of Hajji Baba of Ispahan* (Esfahani's Persian text was probably written in the 1880s, but not published until 1905) as the point of origin of modern story-writing in Iran.[31] The creation of a truly modern prose fiction idiom, as well as the introduction of the short story genre into Persian letters, is more properly attributed to Mohammad `Ali Jamâlzâdeh's collection *Once Upon a Time* (*Yeki bud, yeki nabud*), published in Berlin in 1921.[32] During the 1930s and 1940s, several important collections of short stories were published, mostly by writers who were conversant with and influenced by French, English or German literature. These anthologies, by Sâdeq Hedâyat (*Buried Alive* [*Zendeh be-gur*], 1930; *Three Drops of Blood* [*Seh qatreh khun*], 1932; *Chiaroscuro* [*Sâyeh-ye rowshan*], 1933; *The Stray Dog* [*Sag-e velgard*], 1942), Bozorg `Alavi (*The Suitcase* [*Chamedân*], 1935), once again Jamalzadeh (*The Sanatorium* [*Dâr al-majânin*] and `*Amu Hosayn `Ali*, 1942), Behâzin (*Scatterings* [*Parâkandeh*], 1944), Sâdeq Chubak (*The Puppet Show* [*Khaymeh shab-bâzi*], 1945) and Jalâl Âl-e Ahmad (*The Exchange of Visits* [*Did o bâzdid*], 1946), helped establish the short story as an accepted part of the Persian literary repertoire.[33]

In most of the novels and short stories written during this period, the male writers often cast a victimized woman in the central role of the story, as battered wife or daughter, abandoned and mistreated by men, forced to become a prostitute or live a life of misery.[34] The author employs the condition of these victimized women as a metaphor or symbol for society and, by this means, can register his protest or condemnation of the social and political ills of Iran, without subjecting himself to censorship.[35] Less frequently, women are depicted or experienced by the male character as shrewish or oppressive, as for example in Sadeq Hedayat's *The Blind Owl* (*Buf-e kur*, 1937). In either case, these female roles are more or less stereotypical and do not represent the full humanity of individual women:

> In novel after novel, Iranian writers create and re-create two extreme and worn images of women, that of victims and that of bitches. In both cases the possibility of a meaningful male-female relationship becomes a mere mirage. With the exception of two novels written by women, no real attempt is made to untie the ropes of social protest from the captured images of women, to let the women lead us to whatever buried treasure they have hidden in the depths of their shadowy existence.[36]

As women began to write, the female characters became fuller and their motivations more complex. However, even in the first two outstanding novels written by women, Simin Daneshvar's *Savushun* (1969) and Shahrnush Pârsipur's *The Dog and the Long Winter* (*Sag va zemestân-e boland*, 1976), the attempt to realistically display the life, emotional and physical, of an actual woman is not sustained throughout the length of the novel.[37] Likewise, in most of the novels written since the 1979 Revolution, we encounter only slight development in the fictive image of women. Depictions, for example, of meaningful, multi-dimensional relationships or interactions between men and women are almost wholly lacking.[38] Those novels explicitly consecrated to a woman's search for a place of her own in the fictive realm, a new and authentic way of being female in the changed circumstances of today's Iran--such as Moniru Ravânipur's *Heart of Steel* (*Del-e fulâd*, 1991) and Parsipur's *Tuba and the Meaning of Night* (*Tubâ va ma`nâ-ye shab*)--ultimately fail to create fully real and realized characters.[39] Ironically, stories in which women portray the interior lives of men have achieved greater success in depicting fully-fleshed out characters, as for example Goli Taraqqi's novel *Winter's Sleep* (*Khvâb-e zemestâni*, 1973) and her story "The Strange Habits of Mr. A in Exile" (*Âdât-e gharib-e Âqâ-ye A. dar ghorbat*). In the story included in the present volume,

"A House in the Heavens," Taraqqi presents a character with complex and contradictory emotions, Mahin Banu, whose motivations and whose difficulty in balancing her own needs with those of her children and the expectations of her culture, appear real and believable.

If Iranian women are only now beginning to produce fully-realized female characters, we should recall that women have only recently begun to write professionally in Iran. The memoirs of Tâj al-Saltaneh, a daughter of Nâser al-Din Shâh (r. 1848-96), written in 1924, provide perhaps the first example of a modern prose narrative, though not in this case fiction, in Persian by a woman.[40] The obvious literary abilities of the writer of these memoirs even left some scholars doubting that a woman could have written them, just as the quality of Parvin E`tesami's poems had caused at least one incredulous critic to doubt a woman could be their author.[41] Taj al-Saltaneh, however, did not think favorably of her own powers of expression in comparison with her apparent literary models:

> I wish I were a competent writer like Victor Hugo or
> Monsieur Rousseau and could write this history in
> sweet and delightful language. Alas, I can write but
> simply and poorly.[42]

Perhaps this sense of insecurity inhibited more Iranian women from publishing the results of their literary endeavors and contributing to the creation of a modern prose idiom.

A half-century ago, in 1945, Zahrâ Khânlari published her short story, *Gowhar*, the first example of Persian prose fiction by an Iranian woman to appear in a major literary periodical.[43] Two years later, Simin Daneshvar's collection of stories, *Fire Quenched* (*Âtash-e khâmush*), was published in limited numbers. These stories stand on their own merit, but one might note that both these women were married to influential intellectuals and writers, just as other Iranian women writers and poets (e.g., Parvin E`tesami, Goli Taraqqi, Simin Behbahâni) were the daughters of publishers and intellectuals, and hence had early encouragement, as well as a ready venue for publication of their literary efforts. However, Iranian women coming of age in the period after World War

Two could look for inspiration and assistance to a number of female role models and mentors, such as Amineh Pâkravân, Professor of French Language and Literature and the author of novels in French, as well as Fâtemeh Sayyâh, Professor of Russian Language and Literature and Comparative Literature, both at the University of Tehran.[44]

By the 1970s, a small number of Iranian women had won reputations as promising or successful writers. Since that time, the number of women writing in Iran has increased dramatically, and among the novelists who have enjoyed commercial and critical success with Iranian readers, a number of women stand out, including not only Daneshvar, Mahshid Amirshahy, Goli Taraqqi, Shahrnush Pârsipur, and Ghazâleh `Alizâdeh[45] -- all of whom established their reputation in the later Pahlavi era--but also more recent arrivals on the literary scene, such as Moniru Ravânipur, Farideh Golbu, Mehri Yalfâni, etc., whose work has been recognized since 1979.[46] A number of women writers who flourished from the 1950s through the 70s are no longer active, having either ceased writing or fallen from favor.[47] Since the Islamic Revolution, however, the number of women publishing stories and novels has increased dramatically. Although concern for women's issues kept appearing and reappearing eighty to ninety years ago as a focal theme in the various journals, pamphlets, poems and books published during the Constitutional Revolution, this concern was expressed mostly by men. In the last two decades, women themselves have become active participants in the debates over these questions, and the various attitudes reflected by and about women in Iranian fiction have grown at once more self-aware and less self-conscious, more sophisticated, less overtly concerned with political ideology, and more concerned with the social and cultural experiences of women.

An in-depth discussion of the history of modern Persian prose or even the short story is well beyond the scope of this introduction; for this purpose interested readers can turn to a number of other sources.[48] It should be noted, however, that in twentieth century Iran, literature has played an especially important role in shaping and giving expression to the volatile political issues of the day. Above and beyond issues of style, writers were often viewed in terms of their political commitment—such as the communist party member Bozorg `Alavi, or the anti-imperialist, pro-Islamic Jalâl Âl-e Ahmad—and, as in the Soviet Union, political writers often resorted to allegorical or symbolical methods of critique in order to avoid the Shah's censors.[49] It is worth noting that a woman, Fatemeh Sayyah, was one of the first critics in Iran to expound in a coherent way the importance or even primacy of ideology in literary works, in a brief she delivered for the Soviet model of "socialist realism" at the first Congress of Iranian Writers, held under the sponsorship of the Iran-Soviet Society in 1946.[50]

The number of novels and stories written in Iran which are overtly engaged with political issues or express opposition appears to have diminished under the Islamic Republic of Iran,[51] though critiques, both oblique and direct, of the social conditions in Iran and the eight-year war with Iraq have continued to appear, along with stories criticizing the politics of the Pahlavi regime. Iranians living abroad, naturally, feel more at liberty to critique the politics of the Islamic Republic directly. Even for such expatriate writers, though, the social changes taking place in Iran seem to attract greater interest than the political, as in Mahshid Amirshahy's novel *At Home* (*Dar hazar*, 1987). Of course, there are now, as always, writers more concerned with questions of literary aesthetics than politics or social conditions.

Women and Literature Since the Revolution of 1979

It is too early to evaluate the place of women in post-revolutionary Iranian literature—either in terms of the female characters portrayed, or in terms of the role of women authors; as yet, few critical evaluations of post-revolutionary literature or biographies of literary figures have been written,[52] though Farzaneh Milani's *Veils and Words*, a history of women's fiction writing and its reception in Iran, has provided the basis upon which such a study might be written.[53] A brief catalog of the images of and themes about women appearing in literary works during the first ten years after the Iranian Revolution has also appeared.[54] Works by other scholars have traced the development of fiction writing by Arab women, and would provide interesting comparative material for anyone wishing to trace the effects of twentieth-century social and political upheavals in the Middle East on literature and, specifically, literature written by or about women.[55] Another study, *Woman's Body, Woman's Word* by Fedwa Malti-Douglas, provides a feminist analysis of the literature of Islamic countries, generally.[56]

Despite censorship,[57] paper shortages and other hardships brought on by the war with Iraq, statistics indicate that books are one of the few commodities the production of which has increased since the Islamic Revolution. In the year 1988-9 a record 6300 new titles (excluding text-books) were reportedly published in Iran.[58] Among Islamic feminists, in addition to the works of religious figures such as Ayatollah Khomeini, Ayatollah Motahhari and `Ali Shari`ati, the reading of literary works remains an important intellectual and political pastime. However, it is no longer the works by Iranian writers and intellectuals formerly held in high esteem prior to the Revolution, such as Sadeq Hedayat and Sadeq Chubak (who are not considered sufficiently politically committed), or Samad Behrangi (who was committed, but to the "wrong"—Marxist—politics), but rather the European writers who, even during the reign of the Shah, were canonized as engagé, and whose reputations have not been sullied by involvement in Iranian politics: Dostoevski, Victor Hugo, Camus, Simone de Beauvoir. The appeal of Oriana Falacci, a journalist and novelist focussed on the Middle East who elicited male chauvinist comments from Mohammad Reza Shah during an interview, is not hard to understand. The reasons for the inclusion of Daphné du Maurier among the authors read by Islamic feminists are, however, somewhat less transparent.[59]

Popular among the Iranian literati, though not necessarily the devoutly religious, Gabriel García Márquez, a third-world novelist and 1982 Nobel Prize winner, has created a vogue among certain post-revolutionary Iranian writers for the Magical Realist style.[60] Perhaps the involvement of Latin American countries in anti-colonial struggles against the United States contributes to the appeal of Magical Realism in Iran; otherwise, witches, fairies and magic, though they do play a role in Persian fairy tales, are mostly absent from Persian literature, with the possible exception of the miracles (*karâmât*) related in the medieval *vitae* of Sufis.[61] Ironically, Salman Rushdie, another notable practitioner of Magical Realism, achieved considerable acclaim in the Islamic Republic of Iran for his novel *Midnight's Children*, published in 1981 prior to the appearance of his *Satanic Verses* (1988), which elicited the condemnation of many Muslims and the notorious fatwâ of Ayatollah Khomeini calling for his murder. Naguib Mahfouz, in spite of the 1988 Nobel Prize and his status as a celebrated third-world writer, has not been widely translated in Iran, perhaps because of his outspoken support for the Egyptian-Israeli peace accord.

Exile, either as a theme or a psychological reality, also figures prominently in the writing of Iranians who have chosen to live outside the country.[62] Many authors either left Iran or found it impossible to return due to the political, religious and social conditions prevailing in the Islamic Republic. Some works written since the Revolution, such as Esmâ`il Fassih's *Sorayya in a Coma*, Esmâ`il Kho'i's poem on his return to Bergio Verezzi, Mahshid Amirshahy's *At Home*, and Goli Taraqqi's "The Strange Habits of Mr. A in Exile," deal explicitly with these themes, while exile figures more obliquely in the works of other emigre writers. Still other authors, such as Nahid Rachlin (*Foreigner*) and Taghi Modarressi (*The Pilgrim's Rules of Etiquette*) now write in English from the perspective of Iranian expatriates who have taken root in their new countries. The stories by Shokuh Mirzâdegi, Mahkâmeh Rahimzâdeh and Goli Taraqqi in the present collection directly address the question of Iranian accommodation to the cultures they inhabit outside their homeland.

So how has the Revolution impacted modern Persian literature generally and women's literature in particular? Michael Hillmann, writing in 1988, felt that the Revolution had not caused a major transformation in the "Pahlavi-era modes of fiction," other than that the novel had supplanted the short story as the pre-eminent fictive form.[63] However, the writers he cites as continuing the pre-Revolutionary traditions—all of them men— have, perhaps, been supplanted somewhat by the women authors who began their careers prior to or even since the Revolution.

The Islamic Republic has suppressed the female singing voice, so that singers like Gugush and Parisâ who had achieved commercial success in the 1970s are no longer permitted to perform publicly where men might hear them, nor to make recordings. Ironically, however, in the decade since the Revolution, the female voice is "heard" more and more in stories and novels; between the winters of 1983 and 1985, 126 books by or about women were published and, though the rates of illiteracy among women continue to be higher than those among men, the overall rate of literacy for women has now reached 52%,[64] so the potential audience for stories by women has grown. Likewise, though female actresses must appear always veiled, forcing directors to avert the camera's gaze from the female characters and relegate them to the background,[65] nevertheless, since the Revolution, "more women directors of feature films have emerged in a single decade than in all the decades of film-making preceding the revolution."[66]

Why This Collection?

There has, in recent years, been a proliferation of publications by and about women writers the world over, including anthologies of short stories, novels and works of criticism,[67] many of which specifically set out to redress centuries of relative obscurity. As can be seen from the accompanying list of English translations, relatively few prose works by Iranian women have as yet been rendered into English, and many of the existing translations are neither well-known nor easily obtained. One volume devoted to prose fiction by Iranian women, including 14 stories, *A Walnut Sapling on Masih's Grave*, contains, with one exception, stories written prior to the 1979 Revolution or in the first two years immediately following. The one collection devoted specifically to stories by Iranian women written since the enormous political and social upheavals of the revolution is now out of print.[68] In recent years a number of scholars have attempted to recover the history of Iranian women and narrate their life stories and collective experience.[69] Paradoxically, fiction can often illuminate the realities of daily life and lived experience better than a narrative of historical facts and salient events. The present collection of stories will therefore prove of interest to those wishing to understand the history of women in Iran since the Revolution-- their daily lives, the social issues confronting them and the intellectual, ethical and aesthetic concerns with which they are grappling.

The collection also illustrates some important developments in modern Persian literature. For one thing, as noted above, there are many more women writing than before. This can, in part, be explained by the sheer increase in population and by the apparent increase in literacy among women and men throughout Iran, especially in the villages.[70] The increased popularity of reading among urban Iranians may also stem in part from the fact that many types of popular entertainment during the Shah's regime, such as night-clubs and television programming, have been virtually eliminated, though it should be noted that the Iranian film industry has made great strides forward since the Revolution, both in technical and artistic quality, and that officially discouraged or prohibited western films and television programs are widely distributed and watched throughout Iran, despite recent laws against the use of satellite dishes.

We have selected the stories featured here from a wide variety of published sources, including a dozen different Persian-language journals published in Iran, North America and Europe, in addition to book-length collections of short stories. As one might expect, these stories represent a range of interests and concerns on the part of a variety of women writing in Persian. Some well-known names are missing, either because individual collections of their stories have already been made available to English-speaking readers--Simin Daneshvar (in the collections *Daneshvar's Playhouse* and *Sutra & Other Stories*) and Mahshid Amirshahy (*Suri & Co.: Tales of a Persian Teenage Girl*)--and/or because they have not published short stories, insofar as we have been able to ascertain, since 1979 (Ghazâleh `Alizâdeh).[71] This has allowed room for a sampling of newer writers whose careers were launched only since the Revolution (e.g., Faribâ Vafi, Mehri

Yalfâni, etc.). Some of the stories are overtly feminist ("the Loom"), others deal with the interaction between the sexes ("We Only Fear the Future"), others with girlhood in mid-twentieth century Iran ("The Garden of Sorrow"). The problem of Iranian identity in exile ("The Young John") or the loss of a close-knit sense of family and homeland experienced by Iranians living in diaspora ("A House in the Heavens," "The Pink Room") are recurring themes in a number of the stories. All of the stories, however, focus in some important way on female characters, giving them a voice and an identity, whether it is strong and independent or suppressed by others around them or by social circumstances, thus allowing them to speak in a voice of their own.

As the poetess Tâhereh Saffârzâdeh has claimed, "Good poets are the most honest historians of their times."[72] If that is the case, then these stories, taken together, perhaps tell a larger story about the contemporary history of Iranian women and will constitute a new chapter in the history of Persian letters.

Notes

1. See Fritz Meier, *Die Schöne Mahsati: ein Beitrag zur Geschichte des persischen Vierzeilers* (Wiesbaden: Franz Steiner, 1963).
2. *Divân-e Makhfi, Zib al-Nesâ Beygom*, ed. Ahmad Karami (Nashriyât-e Mâ, 1362/1983). See also, *The Diwan of Zeb-un-Nissa: The First Fifty Ghazals*, trans. by Magan Lal and Jessie Duncan Westbrook (London: John Murnay, 1913).
3. See the chapter on her in M. Ishaque, *Four Eminent Poetesses of Iran* (Calcutta: The Iran Society, 1950), the translations in E. G. Browne, *Materials for the Study of the Babi Religion* (Cambridge: Cambridge University Press, 1918), 347-51, and the forthcoming translations of Amin Banani, *Tahereh: A Portrait in Poetry* (Los Angeles: Kalimat Press).
4. See *A Nightingale's Lament: Selections from the Poems and Fables of Parvin E'tesami*, ed. and trans. Heshmat Moayyad and Margaret Madelung, (Costa Mesa, Calif.: Mazda Publishers, 1985); *Divân-e Parvin E'tesâmi*, introduction and bibliography by Heshmat Moayyad, (Costa Mesa, Calif.: Mazda Publishers, 1987); Jalâl Matini, ed., *Iran Shenasi*, special issue on Parvin-e E'tesâmi, *Iran Shenasi* 1, 2 (Summer 1989), and Heshmat Moayyad, ed. *Once a Dewdrop: Essays on the Poetry of Parvin E'tesami* (Costa Mesa, Calif.: Mazda Publishers, 1994).
5. See, for example, *Forugh Farrokhzad: Bride of Acacias*, trans. by. Jascha Kessler and Amin Banani, (Costa Mesa, Calif.: Mazda, 1981); *A Rebirth: Poems by Foroogh Farrokhzaad*, trans. David Martin, with introductory essay by Farzaneh Milani, (Costa Mesa, Calif.: Mazda, 1985); Michael Hillmann, *A Lonely Woman: Forugh Farrokhzad and Her Poetry* (Washington, D.C.: Mage Publishers and Three Continents Press, 1987); also by Hillmann, "An Iranian Finally Speaks as a Woman and as an Individual" in *Iranian Culture: A Persianist View* (New York, 1990), 145-72, and finally,

Hillmann, ed., *Forugh Farrokhzad: A Quarter-Century Later* (*Literature East and West*, 24 [1988]).

6. With the exception of Sâdeq Hedâyat, Farrokhzad has perhaps received more attention, been more frequently studied and more often translated into English than any other modern Iranian writer. Critics and translators have also devoted much attention to Parvin E`tesmi and Simin Daneshvar, both women.

7. `Ali-Akbar Moshir-Salimi, *Zanân-e sokhanvar az yek hezâr sâl-e pish tâ emruz*, 3 vols. (Tehran: `Ali Akbar `Elmi, 1335-7/1956-8) [Persian women writers from a thousand years ago until today], lists 294 poetesses, but only a handful have achieved any significant recognition. For those that have been accepted into the canon, see M. Ishaque, *Four Eminent Poetesses of Iran*.

8. Bibi Khânom Astarâbâdi, *Ma`âyeb al-rejâl*, ed. Afsaneh Najmabadi (Chicago: Midland Press, 1371/1992). See also the edition by Hasan Javadi, Manizheh Mar`ashi and Simin Shekarlu, *Ruyâru'i-ye zan va mard dar `asr-e Qâjâr--do resâleh-ye Ta'dib al-nesvân va Ma`âyeb al-rejâl* (San Jose, Calif.: Kânun-e pazhuhesh-e târikh-e zanân-e Irân and Sherekat-e Jahân, 1992). E. Powys Mathers translated *Ta'dib al-nesvân* as "The Education of Wives" in Volume 3 of the 12-volume series, *Eastern Love* (London: John Rodker, 1927).

9. C.M. Naim, "Prize-Winning Adab: A Study of Five Urdu Books Written in Response to the Allahabad Government Gazette Notification," in *Moral Conduct and Authority: The Place of Adab in South Asian Islam*, ed. Barbara D. Metcalf, 290-314, (Berkeley: Univ. of California Press, 1984). Naim remarks of Nazir Ahmad that his female characters are "amazingly dynamic people, possessing shape and practical minds. In each instance, they are more competent, stronger, and more effective than almost all the male characters" (305).

10. A good example of this religious argument in favor of the education of Muslim women can be found in the Urdu work *Beheshti Zivar* (1906) by Ashraf `Ali Thânawi. See Barbara Daly Metcalf, "Islamic Reform and Islamic Women: Maulânâ Thânawî's *Jewelry of Paradise*," in *Moral Conduct and Authority: The Place of Adab in South Asian Islam*, ed. Barbara D. Metcalf, 184-95.

11. For the text of those sermons (nos. 33-35) concerned primarily with the "woman question," see *Nimeh-ye Digar* 9 (Spring 1989): 101-112 and also, Afsaneh Najmabadi, "A Different Voice: Taj os-Saltaneh" in *Women's Autobiographies in Contemporary Iran,* ed. A. Najmabadi, 17-31, (Cambridge: Center for Middle Eastern Studies of Harvard University, 1990), 19.

12. As an example of the Bâb's teachings on women, see vâhed 8, bâb 10, of his *Bayân-e fârsi.* For an account of Tâhereh's life, see Chapter Seven, "Qurrat al-`Ayn: The Remover of the Veil" (295-331) in Abbas Amanat, *Resurrection and Renewal: The Making of the Babi Movement in Iran, 1844-50* (Ithaca: Cornell University Press, 1989). Amanat points out (304-5) that Tâhereh's influence led to "a nascent feminist consciousness" among the small circle of women gathered around her. Baha'i sources view Tâhereh's execution in 1852 as a defiant testimonial, not only of her belief in the teachings of the Bâb, but also of her commitment to women's emancipation.

13. See the description of this debate in Joseph Zeidan, *Arab Women Novelists: The Formative Years and Beyond* (Albany, N.Y.: State University of New York Press, 1995), 15-20, and Albert Hourani, *Arabic Thought in the Liberal Age, 1798-1939,* 2nd ed. (Cambridge: Cambridge University Press, 1983), 164-70.

14. Cyrus Mir, "*Nasim-e shemâl* va mas'aleh-ye zan dar nehzat -e mashruteh" [*Nasim-e shemâl* and the "Woman Question" during the Constitutional Movement], *Iran Nameh* 11, 3 (Summer 1993): 427-50.

15. On the role of women in the Constitutional Movement and the emergence of Iranian feminism, see Janet Afary, *The Constitutional Revolution of 1906-11: Grassroots Democracy, Social Democracy and the Origins of Feminism* (New York: Columbia University Press, 1996), especially Chapter 7, "The Women's Councils and the Origins of the Women's Movement in Iran." Mangol Bayat-Philipp, "Women and Revolution in Iran, 1905-11," in *Women in the Muslim World,* Lois Beck and Nikki Keddie, eds., 295-308, addresses this issue, as well. For an outline of the political role played by women at the courts of various dynasties that have ruled Iran throughout its history, as well as a synopsis of the 20th century Iranian women's movement, see Guity Nashat,

"Women in Pre-Revolutionary Iran: A Historical Overview," in *Women and Revolution in Iran*, ed. G. Nashat (Boulder, Co.: Westview Press, 1983), 5-35.

16. Sadr al-Din Elâhi, "Tak-negâri-ye yek ruz-nâmeh: *Dânesh*; avvalin ruz-nâmeh-ye fârsi-zabân barâ-ye zanân-e Irâni" [An introduction to the journal *Dânesh*: the first Persian-language journal for Iranian women], *Iran Shenasi* 6, 2 (Summer 1994): 321-44.

17. See Yahyâ Âryanpur, *Az Nimâ tâ ruzegâr-e mâ* (Tehran: Enteshârât-e Zavvâr, 1374/1995) [*From Nimâ to the present day*], 8-13; Farzaneh Milani, *Veils and Word: The Emerging Voices of Iranian Women Writers* (Syracuse: Syracuse University Press, 1992), 29-32; and Mâshâ'llâh Âjudâni, "Darun-mâyeh-hâ-ye she`r-e Mashruteh" [Major themes in the poetry of the period of the Constitutional Revolution], *Iran Nameh* 11, 4 (Fall 1993): 621-46.

18. See *Star of the West (Najm-e bâkhtar)*, v. 2, nos. 7-8 (August 1, 1911), 7-9 and 11-12 in the Persian section (reprint, Oxford: George Ronald, 1978). She arrived in the U.S. on June 3, 1911 and gave a talk in English to the Persian-American Educational in Washington, D.C., as a result of which she was invited to the silver jubilee anniversary celebration of President and Mrs. William Howard Taft at the White House on June 19, 1911.

19. See Badro'l-Moluk Bamdad, *From Darkness into Light: Women's Emancipation in Iran*, trans. F.R.C. Bagley (Hicksville, N.Y.: Exposition-University, 1977).

20. Hammed Shahidian, "The Iranian Left and the `Woman Question`," *International Journal of Middle Eastern Studies* 26, 2 (May 1994), 224.

21. For the history of this practice, see Shahla Haeri, *The Law of Desire: Women and Temporary Marriage in Shi'i Iran* (Syracuse: Syracuse University Press, 1989).

22. Shahla Haeri, "Temporary Marriage: an Islamic Discourse on Female Sexuality in Iran," in *In the Eye of the Storm*, ed. Mahnaz Afkhami and Erika Friedl, 98-114, (Syracuse, N.Y.: Syracuse University Press, 1994).

23. See the two appendices to *Women in the Eye of the Storm*, ed. Mahnaz Afkhami and Erika Friedl, on "The Legal Status of

Women in the Family in Iran" and "The Islamic Penal Code of the Islamic Republic of Iran: Excerpts Relating to Women."

24. Farah Azari, "The Post-Revolutionary Women's Movement in Iran," in *Women of Iran: The Conflict with Fundamental Islam*, edited by Farah Azari (London: Ithaca Press, 1983), 190.

25. See Marcia Hermansen, "Fatimeh as a Role Model in the Works of Ali Shari`ati," in *Women and Revolution in Iran*, ed. Guity Nashat, 87-96.

26. Azari, "Islam's Appeal to Women in Iran: Illusions and Reality," in *Women of Iran*, 17-21.

27. For a discussion of the station of women in pre-Islamic Iran, see Banafsheh Hejâzi, *Zan beh zann-e târikh* [*The history of attitudes towards women*] (Tehran: Enteshârât-e Shahr Âb, 1370/1991).

28. See Heshmat Moayyad, "Maryam va Shirin dar she`r-e Ferdowsi va Nezâmi" [A comparison of the image of two women, Maryam and Shirin, in the poetry of Ferdowsi and Nezami], *Iranshenasi* 3, 3 (Autumn 1991): 526-39 and Sa`idi Sirjâni, "Zan dar nazar-e Nezâmi" [Nezami's view of Women], *Iranshenasi* 5, 1 (Spring 1993): 105-10; and also his *Simâ-ye do zan: Shirin va Layli dar khamseh-ye Nezâmi-ye Ganjavi* [The visage of two women: Shirin and Layli in the works of Nezâmi] (Tehran: Nashr-e now, 1367/1988). The character Shirin is a fictional representation of a historical Sasanian princess, and she is transformed by Nezâmi into a much more self-willed and independent character than the historical sources suggest. For a discussion of images of female lovers in classical Persian literature, see Shahrokh Meskoob "Maryam-e nâkâm-e `Eshqi va `eshq-e kâmravâ-ye Nezâmi va Khvâju," in *Iran Nameh* 11, 2 (Spring 1993): 283-314. See also the entry on Shirin in the glossary of this book.

29. Erika Friedl, "Women in Contemporary Persian Folktales," in *Women in the Muslim World*, Lois Beck and Nikki Keddie, eds. (Cambridge: Harvard University Press, 1978), 635 and 634.

30. Mary E. Hegland, "Political Roles of Aliabad Women: The Public-Private Dichotomy Transcended," in *Women in Middle Eastern History*, edited by Beth Baron and Nikki Keddie, 215-230 (New Haven: Yale University Press, 1991), 224-5.

31. Hassan Kamshad, *Modern Persian Prose Literature* (Cambridge: Cambridge University Press, 1966), 17-27, who says of Habib-e Esfahâni's *Hajji Baba* that "its style is still followed by modern Persian writers, and it is acclaimed as one of the best compositions of the present century" (27).

32. Michael Hillmann, "Persian Prose Fiction: An Iranian Mirror and Conscience," in *Persian Literature*, ed. Ehsan Yarshater, 291-317 (New York: Persian Heritage Foundation, 1988), 292. For a translation of Jamâlzâdeh's collection, see *Once Upon a Time (Yeki Bud Yeki Nabud)*, trans. by Heshmat Moayyad and Paul Sprachman (Delmar, N.Y.: Caravan Books, 1985).

33. For these writers and their works, see H. Kamshad, *Modern Persian Prose Literature* and Hillmann, "Contemporary Literature of Iran."

34. The oppression or victimization of women in Iran is either a major theme or an important metaphor for government corruption and repression in a wide variety of novels from the 1920s through the 1940s, e.g., Moshfeq Kâzemi's *Frightful Tehran (Tehrân-e makhuf*, 1922); Rabi` Ansâri's *The Crimes of Man (Jenâyât-e bashar*, 1930) about the kidnapping and sale to a brothel of two girls from respectable families; `Abbâs Khalili's novels of the 1920s and 30s; Jahângir Jalili's *I, Too, Have Cried (Man ham geryeh kardeh-am*, 1933); Mohammad Mas`ud's *Diversions of the Night (Tafrihât-e shab*, 1932); Mohammad Hejâzi's *Zibâ* (1931); Jamâlzâdeh's *The Plain of Resurrection (Sahrâ-ye mahshar*, 1947). Sâdeq Hedâyat's relation to and depiction of women has been much discussed. Recently M. R. Ghanoonparvar has addressed the image of women in the fiction of Sâdeq Chubak--"Chand tasvir az zanân dar dâstân-hâ-ye Sâdeq Chubak," *Iranshenasi* 5,2 (Summer 1993): 268-75--where the role of woman as social victim recurs yet again. See the comments on this subject (235-7) of Vidâ Behnâm, "Zan, khânevâdeh va tajaddod" [Women, family and modernization in Iran], *Iran nameh*, 11, 2 (Spring 1993): 227-48.

35. Azar Naficy, "Images of Women in Classical Persian Literature and the Contemporary Iranian Novel," in *In the Eye of the Storm: Women in Post-Revolutionary Iran*, ed. Mahnaz Afkha-

mi and Erika Friedl (Syracuse, N.Y.: Syracuse University Press, 1994), 115-30.

36. A. Naficy, op. cit., 125.

37. A. Naficy, 125.

38. A. Naficy, 127.

39. A. Naficy, 128-9.

40. The memoirs were not published in full in Persian until 1982, *Khâterât-e Tâj al-Saltaneh*, ed. Mansureh Ettehâdiyeh and Sirus Sa`dvandiyân (Tehran: Nashr-e Târikh-e Irân, 1982). On the basis of the autograph manuscript, the editors date the work to 1924. However, as Afsaneh Najmabadi has argued on the basis of internal evidence, Tâj al-Saltaneh probably wrote her memoirs a decade prior to that (See "A Different Voice: Taj os-Saltaneh" in *Women's Autobiographies in Contemporary Iran*, ed. Afsaneh Najmabadi, 17-31, [Cambridge, Mass.: Harvard Center for Middle Eastern Studies, 1990], 21 and 67-8n9). Anna Vanzan and Amin Neshati have translated Taj al-Saltaneh's memoirs into English as: *Crowning Anguish. Taj al-Saltana: Memoirs of A Persian Princess 1884-1914*, ed. Abbas Amanat (Washington, D.C.: Mage Publishers, 1994).

41. Farzaneh Milani, *Veils and Words*, 105-8, and also "Az negâr tâ negârandeh, az maktub tâ kâteb" [From object to subject in literary and visual representation], *Iran Nameh* 12, 1 (Winter 1994), 75.

42. Tâj al-Saltaneh, *Khâterât*, 20. The English translation is by Amin Neshati and Anna Vanzan, in *The Memoirs of Taj al-Saltaneh*, 134.

43. For a translation of this story and a biography of Zahrâ Khânlari, see *A Walnut Sapling on Masih's Grave*, John Green and Farzin Yazdanfar, eds., (Portsmouth, N.H.: Heinemann, 1993), 97-112.

44. Farzaneh Milani, *Veils and Words*, 181.

45. See her collection of four novellas, *Jâddeh-ye kur* [The Blind Highway] (Amir Kabir, 1343/1964).

46. Yalfâni, like Daneshvar before her, is slowly acquiring an international recognition, and her collection of stories and poems, *Parastoo*, was published by the Woman's Press in Toronto in 1995. Note that the late 1970s and 1980s were also a period of

commercial and critical success for female novelists in Greece, including Maro Douka, Eugenia Fakinou, Margarita Karapanou and Alki Zei. See Karen Van Dyck, "Reading Between Worlds: Contemporary Greek Women's Writing and Censorship," *PMLA* 109, 1 (January 1994): 45-60.

47. Any list of women writers before the Revolution would include: Mahin Tavallali (active in the 1950s), Maymanat Dânâ (fl. 1950s-60s), Khâtereh Parvâneh (active in the 60s, also as a singer of traditional Persian music), Shahlâ Latifi and Mahvash Nabavi (who both published in the 1970s), etc.

48. See, for example, in English, Heshmat Moayyad's "The Persian Short Story: An Overview" in *Stories from Iran: A Chicago Anthology 1921-91*, edited by H. Moayyad (Washington, D.C.: Mage Publishers, 1991), 13-29, and also Hassan Kamshad, *Modern Persian Prose Literature* (Cambridge: Cambridge University Press, 1966). In Persian, see Hasan `Âbedini, *Sad sâl dâstân-nevisi dar Irân* [*A hundred years of story-writing in Iran*], 2 vols. (Tehran: Nashr-e Tondar, 1368/1989); Rezâ Barâheni, *Qesseh-nevisi* [*Story-writing*] (Tehran: Enteshârât-e Ashrafi, 1348/1969); `Ali Akbar Kasmâ'i, *Barkhi az nevisandegân-e pishgâm dar dâstân-nevisi-ye emruz-e Irân* [*A few of the early authors who wrote short stories in Iran*] (Sherkat-e Mo'allefân va Motarjemân-e Irân, 1363/1984); Jamâl Mir Sâdeqi, *Qesseh, dâstân-e kutâh, român* [*The tale, the short story and the novel*] (Tehran: Enteshârât-e Âgâh, 1360/1981) and Mohammad `Ali Sepânlu, *Nevisandegân-e pishrov-e Irân* [*Pioneering writers of Iran*] (Tehran: Ketâb-e Zamân, 1362/1983).

49. See M. Hillmann, "The Modernist Trend in Persian Literature and Its Social Impact," *Iranian Studies* 15, 1-4 (1982): 7-29; M.R. Ghanoonparvar, *Prophets of Doom: Literature as a Socio-Political Phenomenon in Modern Iran* (Lanham, Md.: University Press of America, 1984); Hamid Dabashi, "The Poetics of Politics: Commitment in Modern Persian Literature," *Iranian Studies* 18, 2-4 (Spring-Autumn 1985): 147-188, and, in Persian, the article by Mohammad-`Ali Eslâmi-Nodushan, "Chand nokteh-ye goftani va nâ-goftani dar-bâreh-ye adab-e mo`âser-e Irân" [*A few points about modern Persian literature*], *Iranshenasi* 1, 4 (Winter 1990): 649-74.

50. Âzar Naficy, "Dâstân-e bi-pâyân" [A never-ending story] *Iran Nameh* 12, 1 (Winter 1994): 174-7. The title of Sayyâh's talk was "The responsibility of Criticism in Literature," printed in a collection of her articles, *Majmu`eh-ye maqâlât va taqrirât*.

51. There are some notable exceptions within Iran, such as Sa`idi Sirjâni, who died in the custody of the Iranian government.

52. See, however, Ahmad Karimi-Hakkak, "Revolutionary Posturing: Iranian Writers and the Iranian Revolution of 1979," *International Journal of Middle Eastern Studies* 23 (1991), 507-31 and Hillmann's biography of Forugh Farrokhzâd, *A Lonely Woman*, 147-54.

53. Farzaneh Milani, *Veils and Words: The Emerging Voices of Iranian Women Writers* (Syracuse: Syracuse University Press, 1992). See also her article, "Az negâr tâ negârandeh, az maktub tâ kâteb" [From object to subject in literary and visual representation], *Iran Nameh* 12, 1 (Winter 1994): 51-80.

54. Zahrâ Zavvâriân, *Tasvir-e zan dar dah sâl dâstân-nevisi-ye enqelâb-e Eslâmi* [The image of woman in stories written in the ten years after the Islamic Revolution] (Tehran: Howzeh-ye Honari-ye Sâzmân-e Tablighât-e Eslâmi, 1370/1991).

55. See, for example, Evelyne Accad, *Sexuality and War: Literary Masks in the Middle East* (New York: New York University Press, 1990); Leila Ahmed, *Women and Gender in Islam: Historical Roots of a Modern Debate* (New Haven: Yale University Press, 1992); Miriam Cooke, "Telling Their Lives: A Hundred Years of Arab Women's Writings," *World Literature Today* 60 (Spring 1986): 212-6; and *War's Other Voices: Women Writers on the Lebanese Civil War* (Cambridge: Cambridge University Press, 1987); Mona Fayad, *The Road to Feminism: Arab Women Writers* (East Lansing: Michigan State University, 1987); and Joseph Zeidan, *Arab Women Novelists: The Formative Years and Beyond* (Albany: State University of New York Press, 1995).

56. Fedwa Malti-Douglas, *Woman's Body, Woman's Word: Gender and Discourse in Arabo-Islamic Writing* (Princeton: Princeton University Press, 1991).

57. For the history of censorship after the Islamic Revolution, see Gholâm-Hosayn Sâ`edi, "*Farhang-koshi va honar-zodâ'i dar*

Jomhuri-ye Eslâmi" [*Culture-cide and the eradication of art in the Islamic Republic*], *Alef-bâ*, n.s. 1 (Winter 1361/1983): 1-8.

58. Karim Emâmi, *"Nashr-e ketâb dar Irân ba`d az enqelâb"* [*The publication of books in Iran since the Revolution*] *Fasl-e ketâb* 7 (vol. 3, no. 1, Spring 1991): 120-2.

59. Fariba Adelkhah, *La révolution sous le voile: Femmes islamiques d'Iran* (Paris: Éditions Karthala, 1991), 222-4.

60. See Hurâ Yâvari, *"Nâ-hamzamâni-ye dâstân va ensân"* [Reflections on the influence of Gabriel García Márquez on three Persian novels written since the Revolution], *Iran Nameh* 9, 4 (Autumn 1991): 635-43.

61. The relationship between Magical Realism and the miracles of Sufi saints is made explicit in a recent prize-winning film by Dâryush Mehrju'i, "Pari," the script of which is adapted, oddly enough, from J.D. Salinger's *Franny and Zooey*.

62. See the critical bibliography for articles by Michael Beard, Mohammad Mehdi Khorrami and Nasrin Rahimieh in this regard.

63. Hillmann, "Persian Prose Fiction," op. cit., 317.

64. Akbar Aghajanian, "The Status of Women and Female Children in Iran: An Update from the 1986 Census," in *In the Eye of the Storm*, 44-60, ed. by Mahnaz Afkhami and Erika Friedl (see, specifically, the charts on 45-46). Note that this figure represents an increase from the data for 1976, three years prior to the Revolution, when only 35.5% of women were reported as literate. Thus, there has been a highly significant increase in the literacy rate for women, and the gap between men and women has narrowed somewhat. While the literacy numbers have increased for women and the percentage of girls attending primary school has risen appreciably in urban and especially rural areas, the percentage of girls attending high school in 1986 had dropped significantly from the number attending in 1976 (p. 47).

65. Hamid Naficy, "Zan va neshâneh shenâsi-ye hejâb va negâh dar sinemâ-ye Irân" [Women and the semiotics of veiling and vision in Iranian cinema], *Iran Nameh* 9, 3 (Summer 1991): 411-24.

66. Hamid Naficy, "Veiled Vision/Powerful Presences: Women in Post-revolutionary Iranian Cinema," in *In the Eye of the Storm*, 131-50, ed. Mahnaz Afkhami and Erika Friedl, 131.

67. Among the many examples are Susie Tharu and K. Lalita, *Women Writing in India: 600 B.C. To the Present*, 2 vols, (NY: Feminist Press 1993); *The Slate of Life: More Contemporary Stories by Women Writers of India* (Feminist Press 1990 and 94); *Unmapped Territories: New Women's Fiction From Japan*, ed. Yukiko Tanaka (Seattle: Women In Translation, 1991); *An Arabian Mosaic: Short Stories by Arab Women Writers*, ed. and trans. by Dalya Cohen-Mor (Potomac, Md.: Sheba Press, 1993).

68. *Stories by Iranian Women Since the Revolution*, trans. by Sorayya Sullivan (Austin, Texas: Center for Middle Easter Studies, University of Texas, 1991).

69. See, inter alia, *Women and Revolution in Iran*, ed. Guity Nashat; *In the Eye of the Storm*, ed. Mahnaz Afkhami and Erika Friedl; *Women's Autobiography in Iran*, ed. Afsaneh Najmabadi; Janet Afary, *The Iranian Constitutional Revolution*; Haideh Moghissi, *Feminism and Populism in Iran*, as well as periodicals devoted to women's history, such as *Nimeh-ye Digar*.

70. See the statistics in *Women in Revolutionary Iran*, ed. G. Nashat.

71. The following authors and the titles of their works represent further examples of fiction written by women since the 1979 Revolution. Although we found bibliographical citations for these works, we have been unable to locate copies and it is not clear in every case whether the books cited are novels or short story collections: Mahin Afkham Rasuli (*Chahârdah dâstân*, 1978-9), Ghazâleh `Alizâdeh (*Do manzareh*, 1363/1984), Malikeh Baqâ'i-Kermâni (b. 1914, *Shekasteh bâlân*, 1363/1984), Susan Ardekâni (*Dar gozargâh-e zendegi*, 1371/1992), Shivâ Arestu'i (*U râ ke didam zibâ shodam*, 1372/1993), Âzitâ Âzmun (*Takyeh bar shâkheh-hâ-ye gham*, 1371/1992), Manizheh Ârmin (*Român-e sorud-e arvandrud*, 1368/1989; *Râz-e lahzeh-hâ*, 1372/1993), Semirâ Aslânpur (*Majmu`eh-ye kuh-hâ-ye âsemân*, 1368/1989), Farkhondeh Âqâ'i (*Majmu`eh-hâ-ye tapeh-hâ-ye sabz*, 1366/1987), etc.

72. From *Harakat va diruz* (Tehran: Enteshârât-e Ravâq, 1357/1979), 162, as cited and translated by Farzaneh Milani,

"Revitalization: Some Reflections on the Work of Saffar-Zadeh,"
129.

I. A Bibliography of Stories and Novels by Iranian Women Translated into English

Abbasi, Farahnaz, "The Mirror," trans. by Farzin Yazdanfar, in Heshmat Moayyad, ed., *Stories from Iran: A Chicago Anthology, 1921-1991* (Washington, D.C.: Mage Publishers, 1991), 553-5.

Abtahi, Fatimah, "A Walnut Sapling on Masih's Grave," trans. by John Green in John Green and Farzin Yazdanfar, eds., *A Walnut Sapling on Masih's Grave and Other Stories by Iranian Women* (Portsmouth, New Hampshire: Heinemann, 1993), 1-11.

_____ "A Young Walnut on the Messiah's Grave," trans. by Sorayya Sullivan, in *Stories by Iranian Women Since the Revolution* (Austin, Tx: Center for Middle Eastern Studies at the University of Texas at Austin: 1991), 71-9.

Amirshahy [Amirshahi], Mahshid, *Suri & Co.: Tales of a Persian Teenage Girl* [a collection of short stories], trans. by J.E. Knörzer, with an introduction by Hafez Farmayan, (Austin, TX: Center for Middle Eastern Studies, The University of Texas, 1995).

_____ "String of Beads," trans. by Michael Beard. *Edebiyat* 3 (1978): 1-9.

_____ "The End of the Passion Play", trans. by Minoo Southgate and Bjorn R. Rye, in Minoo Southgate, ed., *Modern Persian Short Stories* (Washington, D.C: Three Continents Press, 1980), 161-72.

_____ "Brother's Future Family," trans. by Michael Beard, in *Stories from Iran*, 423-31. Also translated as "Big Brother's Future In-Laws" by J.E. Knörzer in *Suri & Co.*, 11-19.

_____ "The Smell of Lemon Peel, the Smell of Fresh Milk," trans. by Heshmat Moayyad, in *Stories from Iran*, 433-45.

_____ "After the Last Day," trans. by John Green, in *A Walnut Sapling on Masih's Grave*, 12-20.

_____ "Peyton Place," trans. by Michael Beard, in *A Walnut Sapling on Masih's Grave*, 22-33. Also translated as "Peyton Place," by J.E. Knörzer in *Suri & Co.*, 68-77.

_____ "My Grandfather, the Grandson of this Gentleman's Mother's Aunt," trans. by J.E. Knörzer in *Suri & Co.*, 20-28.

_____ "The Party," trans. by J.E. Knörzer in *Suri & Co.*, 29-37.

_____ "The Women's Mourning Ceremony," trans. by J.E. Knörzer in *Suri & Co.*, 38-47.

_____ "Naming Simin's Baby," trans. by J.E. Knörzer in *Suri and Co.*, 48-54.

_____ "The Interview," trans. by J.E. Knörzer in *Suri and Co.*, 55-67.

_____ "Paikan Place," trans. by J.E. Knörzer in *Suri and Co.*, 78-87.

Bahrami, Mihan, "Animal," trans. by Sorayya Sullivan in *Stories by Iranian Women*, 138-60.

_____ "Haj Barekallah," trans. by M. R. Ghanoonparvar, in *A Walnut Sapling on Masih's Grave*, 34-61.

Daneshvar, Simin, *Daneshvar's Playhouse: A Collection of Stories*. Trans. by Maryam Mafi (Washington, D.C.: Mage Publishers, 1989). Includes five stories--"The Accident," "The Playhouse," "To Whom Can I Say Hello," "Traitor's Intrigue," and "Vakil's Bazaar," and Daneshvar's memoir of the death of her husband, Jalâl Al-e Ahmad, "Loss of Jalal."

_____ "The Half-Closed Eye," trans. by Frank Lewis, in *Stories from Iran: A Chicago Anthology, 1921-1991*, ed. Heshmat Moayyad, 125-43.

_____ "A Land like Paradise," trans. by Minoo Southgate and Bjorn R. Rye, in Minoo Southgate, ed., *Modern Persian Short Stories* (Washington, D.C: Three Continents Press, 1980), 34-52.

_____ *A Persian Requiem*, trans. by Roxane Zand (New York: George Brazillier, 1992). [A second translation of *Savushun*]

_____ *Savushun: A Novel About Iran*, trans. by M.R. Ghanoonparvar. (Washington, D.C.: Mage Publishers, 1990).

_____ "The Story of a Street," trans. by John Green, in *A Walnut Sapling on Masih's Grave*, 62-81.

_____ *Sutra and Other Stories*, trans. by Hasan Javadi and Amin Neshati (Washington, D.C.: Mage Publishers, 1994). Includes six stories: "Anis," "Bibi Shahr Banu," "A City Like Paradise" [the second translation of this story], "Model," "Shards" and "Sutra."

_____ "Traitor's Deceit," trans. by Sorayya Sullivan, in *Stories by Iranian Women*, 16-35. [A second translation of "Kayd al-Khâ'enin"].

Dowlatâbâdi, Mahdokht, "Scapegoat," trans. by Sorayya Sullivan, in *Stories by Iranian Women*, 114-125.

Ettehad, Nasrin, "A Veil with Tiny Aster Flowers," trans. by Sorayya Sullivan, in *Stories by Iranian Women*, 173-84.

Ghazinur, Ghodsi, "Aboud's Drawings," trans. by Sorayya Sullivan, in *Stories by Iranian Women*, 87-99.

Kashkuli, Mahdokht, "The Button," trans. by Sorayya Sullivan, in *Stories by Iranian Women*, 51-57.

_____ "Congratulations and Condolences," trans. by Franklin Lewis, in *A Walnut Sapling on Masih's Grave*, 83-96.

Khanlari, Zahra, "Gowhar," trans. by John Green, in *A Walnut Sapling on Masih's Grave*, 97-111.

Kuhi, Fereshteh, "Mrs. Ahmadi's Husband," trans. by Sorayya Sullivan in *Stories by Iranian Women*, 161-72.

Mirzadegi, Shokouh, "The Starling Spring," trans. by John Green, in *A Walnut Sapling on Masih's Grave*, 113-27.

[*Modern Persian Short Stories*, edited by Minoo Southgate (Washington, D.C: Three Continents Press, 1980)].

Natiq, Huma, "A Visit with the Children in the Upper Village," trans. by John Green, in *A Walnut Sapling on Masih's Grave*, 128-39.

Nikzad, Giti, "The Tale of the Rabbit and the Tomatoes," trans.by Farzin Yazdanfar, in *A Walnut Sapling on Masih's Grave*, 140-2.

Parsipur, Shahrnush, "Sara," trans. by Farzin Yazdanfar, in *A Walnut Sapling on Masih's Grave*, 143-9.

_____ "Trial Offers," trans. by Paul Sprachman, in *Stories from Iran*, 485-529.

Rahmani, A. [a pseudonym], "A Short Hike," trans. by Sorayya Sullivan in *Stories by Iranian Women*, 126-137.

Ravanipur, Moniru, "The Future Is All We Fear," trans. by Afshin Nassiri, in *Chanteh: The Iranian Cross-Cultural Quarterly*, no. 4, summer 1993, 14-17.

_____ "The Long Night," trans. by John R. Perry, in *Stories from Iran*, 533-41.

Riahi, Lyly, "The Cactus Flower," trans. by Sorayya Sullivan, in *Stories by Iranian Women*, 36-49.

Sazgar, Zhila, "There is no Truth," trans. by John Green, in *A Walnut Sapling on Masih's Grave*, 151-6.

Shahriari, Mojdeh, "The Girl in the Rose Scarf," trans. by Sorayya Sullivan, *Stories by Iranian Women*, 100-113.

Shahrzad, "Me...Want...Candy," trans. by Sorayya Sullivan, in *Stories by Iranian Women*, 80-86.

[*Stories by Iranian Women Since the Revolution*, translated by Sorayya Sullivan (Austin, Tex.: Center for Middle Eastern Studies, the University of Texas, Austin, 1991)].

[*Stories from Iran: A Chicago Anthology, 1921-1991*, edited by Heshmat Moayyad (Washington, D.C.: Mage Publishers, 1991)].

Taraghi [Taraqqi], Goli, "The Great Lady of My Soul: A Story," trans. by Faridoun Farrokh, *Iranian Studies* 15 (1982): 211-25; also in *A Walnut Sapling on Masih's Grave*, 157-71.

_____ "The Great Lady of My Soul," trans. by Sorayya Sullivan, in *Stories By Iranian Women*, 58-70.

_____ "Aziz Aqa's Gold Filling," trans. by Farzin Yazdanfar and Frank Lewis, in *Stories from Iran*, 405-419.

_____ "A Place in the Sky," trans. by Maryam Mafi, in *Chanteh:The Iranian Cross-Cultural Quarterly*, no. 2, Winter 1993, 9-17.

_____ "Someday," trans. by John Green, in *A Walnut Sapling on Masih's Grave*, 173-84.

_____ *Winter Sleep*, Goli Taraqqi, translated by Francine Mahak (Mazda, 1994).

_____ "The Wolf Lady," trans. by Faridoun Farrokh, in *Chaneh:The Iranian Cross-Cultural Quarterly*, no. 6, Winter/Spirng 1994, 20-25.

[*A Walnut Sapling on Masih's Grave and Other Stories by Iranian Women*, ed. by John Green and Farzin Yazdanfar (Portsmouth, New Hamp.: Heinemann, 1993)].

Yalfâni, Mehri, *Parastoo: Stories and Poems* (Toronto: Women's Press, 1995).

II. A Select Bibliography of Studies on Women and Writing in Iran and the Middle East

`Âbedini, Hasan, *Sad sâl dâstân-nevisi dar Irân* [One hundred years of story-writing in Iran], 2 vols., 2nd ed., (Tehran: Nashr-e Tondar, 1369-70/1989-90).

_____ "Român va dâstân az 58 tâ 72" [Stories and novels from 1979-1993) *Gardun* 46-7, 128-35.

Accad, Evelyne, *Sexuality and War: Literary Masks in the Middle East* (New York: New York University Press, 1990).

Adelkhah, Fariba, *La révolution sous le voile: Femmes islamiques d'Iran* (Paris: Éditions Karthala, 1991).

Afkhami, Mahnaz and Erika Friedl, eds. *In the Eye of the Storm: Women in Post-Revolutionary Iran* (Syracuse, N.Y.: Syracuse University Press, 1994).

Ahmed, Leila, *Women and Gender in Islam: Historical Roots of a Modern Debate* (New Haven: Yale University Press, 1992).

Âjudâni, Mâshâ' Allâh, "Darun-mâyeh-hâ-ye she`r-e Mashruteh" [Major themes in the poetry of the period of the Constitutional Revolution], *Iran Nameh* 11, 4 (Fall 1993): 621-46.

Alishan, Leonardo, "Tahereh Saffarzadeh: From the Wasteland to the Imam," in *Iranian Studies*, 15, 1-4 (1982): 181-210.

_____ "Parvin E`tesami, The Magna Mater, and the Culture of the Patriarchs" in *Once a Dewdrop: Essays on the Poetry of Parvin E`tesami*, ed. H. Moayyad (Costa Mesa, Calif.:Mazda, 1994), 20-46.

Allen, Roger, Hilary Kilpatrick and Ed de Moor, eds., *Love and Sexuality in Modern Arabic Literature* (London: Saqi Books, 1995).

Assefi, Nassim, Review of Simin Daneshvar's *A Persian Requiem,* translated by Roxane Zand, *Iranian Studies* 27 (1994): 181-3.

Azari, Farah, ed. *Women of Iran: The Conflict with Fundamentalist Islam* (London: Ithaca Press, 1983).

Bamdad, Badr o'l-Moluk, From Darkness into Light: Women's Emancipation in Iran, trans. F. R. C. Bagley (Hicksville, N.Y.: Exposition-University, 1977).

Barâheni, Rezâ, *Qesseh-nevisi* [Story-writing] (Tehran: Enteshârât-e Ashrafi, 1348/1969).

_____ *Târikh-e mozakkar* [Masculine history] (Tehran: `Elmi, n.d.).

Beard, Michael, "Zan-e tu-ye qatâr: zibâ'i-shenâsi-ye tab`id dar she`r-e `bâz gasht' az Esmâ`il Kho'i" [The woman in the train: the esthetics of exile in Esmâ`il Kho'i's poem "Return"], *Iran Nameh* 9, 1 (Winter 1991): 90-97.

Beard, Michael and Hasan Javadi, "Iranian Writers Abroad," *World Literature* 60, 2 (Spring 1989): 258.

Beck, Lois and Nikki Keddie, eds. *Women in the Muslim World* (Cambridge: Harvard University Press, 1978).

Behbahâni, Simin, "Dar entezâr-e bârân" [Waiting for the rain (a critique of Parsipur's novel *Tuba and the Meaning of Night*)], *Iran Nameh*, 10, 2 (Spring 1992): 358-67.

Behnâm, Vidâ, "Zan, khânevâdeh va tajaddod" [Women, family and modernization in Iran], *Iran Nameh*, 11, 2 (Spring 1993): 227-48.

Cohen-Mor, Dalya, ed. and trans., *An Arabian Mosaic: Short Stories by Arab Women Writers* (Potomac, Md.: Sheba Press, 1993).

Cooke, Miriam, "Arab Women Writers," in *Modern Arabic Literature*, ed. M.M. Badawi, 443-62, (Cambridge: Cambridge University Press, 1992).

_____ "Telling Their Lives: A Hundred Years of Arab Women's Writings," *World Literature Today* 60 (Spring 1986): 212-6

_____ *War's Other Voices: Women Writers on the Lebanese Civil War* (Cambridge: Cambridge University Press, 1987).

Dabashi, Hamid, "The Poetics of Politics: Commitment in Modern Persian Literature," *Iranian Studies* 18, 2-4 (Spring-Autumn 1985): 147-88.

Dâvarân, Fereshteh, "Impersonality in Parvin E`tesami's Poetry," in *Once a Dewdrop: Essays on the Poetry of Parvin E`tesami*, ed. H. Moayyad (Costa Mesa, Calif.: Mazda, 1994), 69-89.

Elâhi, Sadr al-Din, Review of Mehri Yalfâni's *Kasi mi-âyad*, *Iranshenasi* 7, 3 (Autumn 1995): 639-45.

Elwell-Sutton, L.P., "Kissa in Persian Literature," in *Encyclopedia of Islam*, 2nd edition, s.v.

Eslâmi-Nodushan, Mohammad-`Ali, "Chand nokteh-ye goftani va nâ-goftani dar-bâreh-ye adab-e mo`âser-e Irân" [A few observations about modern Persian literature], *Iranshenasi* 1,4 (Winter 1990): 649-74.

Farman Farmaian, Sattareh with Dona Munker, *Daughter of Persia: A Woman's Journey From Her Father's Harem Through the Islamic Revolution* (New York: Anchor Books, 1992).

Farrokh, A., "Beh qalam-e zanân; dar-bâreh-ye zanân" [About women, by women], *Fasl-nâmeh-ye Goftogu, vizheh-ye zanân* (Fall 1374/1995): 133-35.

Farrokh, Faridoun, with M.R. Ghanoonparvar, "Portraits in Exile in the Fiction of Esma'il Fassih and Goli Taraghi," in *Iranian Refugees and Exiles Since Khomeini*, ed. Asghar Fathi, (Costa Mesa, Calif.: Mazda Publishers, 1991), 280-93.

Fayad, Mona, *The Road to Feminism: Arab Women Writers* (East Lansing, Mich.: Michigan State University, 1987).

Fischer, Michael, "On Changing the Concept and Position of Persian Women," in *Women in the Muslim World*, Lois Beck and Nikki Keddie, eds., 189-215, (Cambridge: Harvard University Press, 1978).

Friedl, Erika, "Women in Contemporary Persian Folktales," in *Women in the Muslim World*, Lois Beck and Nikki Keddie, eds., 629-50, (Cambridge: Harvard University Press, 1978).

Ghanoonparvar, M.R., "On Savushun and Simin Daneshvar's Contribution to Persian Fiction," *Iranshenasi* 3, 4 (Winter 1992): 77-88.

_____ "Hushang Golshiri and Post-Pahlavi Concerns of the Iranian Writer of Fiction." *Iranian Studies* 18, 2-4 (Spring-Autumn 1985): 349-73.

_____ *In a Persian Mirror: Images of the West and Westerners in Iranian Fiction* (Austin: University of Texas Press, 1993).

_____ *Prophets of Doom: Literature as a Socio-Political Phenomenon in Modern Iran* (Lanham, Md.: University Press of America, 1984).

_____ Bâ neqâb-e siâh: tahlil-i az se dâstân-e kutâh-e Simin Dâneshvar" [With a black veil: an analysis of three short stories by Simin Daneshvar] *Nimeh-ye Digar* 8 (Fall 1988): 165-79.

_____ "Dam-i bâ *Ahl-e Gharq*" [An overview of Moniru Ravanipur's novel, *The Drowned Folk*], *Iranshenasi* 4, 2
(Summer 1992): 403-7.

_____ "Kand va kâvi dar *Zanân be-dun-e mardân*" [Excavating
Shahrnush Parsipur's novel, *Women without Men*] *Iran
Nameh* 9, 4 (Autumn 1991): 690-9.

_____ "Chand tasvir az zanân dar dâstân-hâ-ye Sâdeq Chubak" [A
few portraits of women in the stories of Sadeq Chubak],
Iranshenasi 5, 2 (Summer 1993): 268-75.

Green, John, *Iranian Short Story Authors: A Bio-bibliographic Sur-
vey* (Costa Mesa, Calif.: Mazda, 1989).

Guppy, Shusha, *The Blindfold Horse: Memories of a Persian Childhood* (Boston: Beacon Press, 1988).

_____ *A Girl in Paris* (London: Heinemann, 1991).

Haeri, Shahla, *The Law of Desire: Women and Temporary Marriage
in Shi'i Iran* (Syracuse: Syracuse University Press, 1989).

_____ "Temporary Marriage: an Islamic discourse on female
Sexuality in Iran," in *In the Eye of the Storm*, ed. Mahnaz
Afkhami and Erika Friedl, 98-114.

Hafez, Sabry, *The Genesis of Arabic Narrative Discourse* (London:
Saqi Books, 1993).

Hejâzi, Banafsheh, *Zan beh zann-e târikh* [The conception of
women in pre-Islamic history] (Tehran: Enteshârât-e Shahr
Âb, 1370/1991).

Hermansen, Marcia, "Fatimeh as a Role Model in the Works of
Ali Shari`ati," in *Women and Revolution in Iran*, ed. Guity
Nashat (Boulder, Co.: Westview Press, 1983), 87-96.

Hillmann, Michael, "Contemporary Literature of Iran," in *Persian Literature*, ed. Ehsan Yarshater (New York: Bibliotheca Persica, 1988).

_____ "The Modernist Trend in Persian Literature and Its Social Impact" *Iranian Studies* 15, 1-4 (1982): 7-29.

_____ "Revolution, Islam and Contemporary Persian Literature," in *Iran: Essays on a Revolution in the Making*, ed. A. Jabbari and R. Olson (Lexington, Ky.: 1981).

Ishaque, M., *Four Eminent Poetesses of Iran* (Calcutta: The Iran Society, 1950).

Kamshad, Hassan, *Modern Persian Prose Literature* (Cambridge: Cambridge University Press, 1966)

Kandiyoti, Deniz, "Slavegirls, Temptresses and Comrades: Images of Women in the Turkish Novel," *Feminist Issues* 8, 1 (Spring 1988): 35-50.

Karimi-Hakkak, Ahmad, *Recasting Persian Poetry: Scenarios of Poetic Modernity in Iran* (Salt Lake City, Ut.: University of Utah Press, 1995).

_____ "Revolutionary Posturing: Iranian Writers and the Iranian Revolution of 1979," *International Journal of Middle Eastern Studies* 23 (1991), 507-31.

Katouzian, Homâ[youn], "Iran" in *Modern Literature in the Near and Middle East, 1850-1970*, ed. Robin Ostle (Routledge: London, 1991), 130-57.

_____ "Zan dar âsâr-e Sâdeq Hedâyat" [Women in the works of Sadeq Hedayat], *Fasl-e Ketâb* 8 (v. 3, #2, Summer 1991): 34-49.

Kasmâ'i, `Ali Akbar, *Barkhi az nevisandegân-e pishgâm dar dâstân-nevisi-ye emruz-e Irân* [Some of the pioneer short-story writers of modern Iran] (Sherkat-e mo'allefân va motar-jemân-e Irân, 1363/1984).

Khorrami, Mohammad Mehdi, "Qesseh va qesseh-nevis dar tab`id: târikhcheh-ye esteqlâl-e adabi" [The story and the story-writer in exile: a history of literary independence], *Iranshenasi* 5, 1 (Spring 1993): 183-94.

Mahak, Francine, "Critical Analysis and Translation of Winter Sleep by Goli Taraghi," (Ph.D. dissertation, University of Utah, 1986).

Malti-Douglas, Fedwa, *Woman's Body, Woman's Word* (Princeton: Princeton University Press, 1991).

Mazâre`i, Mehrnush and Mahdokht San`ati, "Mosâhebeh bâ Shahrnush-e Pârsipur" [Interview with Shahrnush-e Par-sipur], *Forugh* 2:7-8 (Fall 1991): 5-22.

Meisami, Julie, "Iran," in *Modern Literature in the Near and Middle East, 1850-1970*, ed. by Robin Ostle (Routledge: London, 1991), 45-62.

Milani, Farzaneh, "Love and Sexuality in the Poetry of Forugh Farrokhzad: A Reconsideration," *Iranian Studies* 15, 1-4(1982): 117-28.

_____ "Revitalization: Some Reflections on the Work of Saffar-Zadeh," in *Women and Revolution in Iran*, ed. Guity Nashat, 129-40, (Boulder, Col.: Westview Press, 1983).

_____ "Power, Prudence, and Print: Censorship and Simin 47. Daneshvar," *Iranian Studies* 18, 2-4 (Spring-Autumn 1985): 325-

_____ *Veils and Words: The Emerging Voices of Iranian Women Writers* (Syracuse, N.Y.: Syracuse University Press, 1992).

_____ "Az negâr tâ negârandeh, az maktub tâ kâteb" [From object to subject in literary and visual representation], *Iran Nameh* 12, 1 (Winter 1994): 51-80.

_____ "Pâ-ye sohbat-e Shahrnush Pârsipur" [An interview with Shahrnush Parsipur], *Iran Nameh* 11, 4 (Fall 1993): 691-704.

_____ "Judith Shakespeare and Parviz E`tesami," in *Once a Dewdrop: Essays on the Poetry of Parvin E`tesami*, ed. H. Moayyad (Costa Mesa, Calif.: Mazda, 1994), 141-59.

Milani, Farzaneh, ed., *Nimeh-ye Digar (vizheh-ye Simin Dâneshvar)* 8 (1367/1989) [a special issue of the feminist periodical "The Other Half" dedicated to articles about Simin Daneshvar].

Mir Sâdeqi, Jamâl, *Qesseh, dâstân-e kutâh, român* [Fiction, the short story and the novel] (Tehran: Enteshârât-e Âgâh, 1360/1981).

Moayyad, Heshmat, "The Persian Short Story: An Overview" in *Stories from Iran: A Chicago Anthology 1921-91*, ed. H. Moayyad (Washington, D.C.: Mage Publishers, 1991), 13-29.

_____ "Maryam va Shirin dar she`r-e Ferdowsi va Nezâmi" [A comparison of the image of two women, Maryam and Shirin, in the poetry of Ferdowsi and Nezami], *Iranshenasi* 3, 3 (Autumn 1991): 526-39.

_____ "Nasr-e dâstân-nevisi-ye fârsi, morur-i kutâh" [The prose of the Persian short story: a short overview] in *Khusheh-hâ'i az kherman-e honar va adab* #6 (Landegg, Switzerland: Anjoman-e honar va adab, 1995), 259-71.

Moayyad, Heshmat, ed. *Once a Dewdrop: Essays on the Poetry of Parvin E`tesami* (Costa Mesa, Calif.: Mazda Publishers, 1994).

Mosteshar, Cherry, *Unveiled: One Woman's Nightmare in Iran* (New York: St. Martin's Press, 1995).

Mowlavi, Fereshteh, *Ketâb-shenâsi-ye dâstân-e kutâh (Irân va jahân)* [Bibliography of the short story--Iran and the world], (Tehran: Enteshârât-e Nilufar, 1371/1992).

Naficy, Azar, "Images of Women in Classical Persian Literature and the Contemporary Iranian Novel," in *In the Eye of the Storm: Women in Post-Revolutionary Iran*, ed. Mahnaz Afkhami and Erika Friedl, 115-30, (Syracuse, N.Y.: Syracuse University Press, 1994).

Naficy, Hamid, "Veiled Vision/Powerful Presences: Women in Post-revolutionary Iranian Cinema," in *In the Eye of the Storm*, ed. Mahnaz Afkhami and Erika Friedl, 131-50.

_____ "Zan va neshâneh-shenâsi-ye hejâb va negâh dar sinemâ-ye Irân" [Women and the semiotics of veiling and vision in Iranian cinema], *Iran Nameh* 9, 3 (Summer 1991): 411-24.

Najmabadi, Afsaneh, "The Hazards of Modernity and Morality: Women, State and Ideology in Contemporary Iran," in *Women, Islam and the State*, ed. Deniz Kandiyoti (Philadelphia: Temple University Press, 1991).

Najmabadi, Afsaneh, ed., *Women's Autobiographies in Contemporary Iran*, (Cambridge, Mass.: Harvard Center for Middle Eastern Studies, 1991).

Navvâbi, Dâvud, *Târikhcheh-ye tarjomeh az Farânseh be Fârsi dar Irân az âghâz tâ konun* [History of translations from French to Persian from the beginning to the present-day] (Kirman: Dâneshgâh-e Kermân, 1363/1984).

Paidar, Parvin, *Women and the Political Process in Twentieth-Century Iran* (Cambridge [England]; New York: Cambridge University Press, 1995).

Pakzad, Sima, "The Legal Status of Women in the Family in Iran," in *In the Eye of the Storm*, ed. M. Afkhami and E. Friedl, 169-79.

Rahimieh, Nasrin, "Cheguneh mitavân birun az vatan Irâni bud?" [How to be Iranian outside the homeland], *Iran Nameh* 12, 4 (Fall 1994): 541-8.

_____ Review of Goli Taraqqi's *Khâtereh-hâ-ye parâkandeh: majmu`eh-ye qesseh*," in *Iran Nameh* 12, 3 (Summer 1994): 561-564.

_____ Review of *Suri & Co.: Tales of a Persian Teenager*, translated by J.E. Knörzer, in *World Literature Today* 70, 1 (Winter 1996): 234.

Sepânlu, Mohammad `Ali, *Nevisandegân-e pishrov-e Irân* [Pioneering writers of Iran] (Tehran: Ketâb-e Zamân, 1362/1983).

Sirjâni, Sa`idi, "Zan dar nazar-e Nezâmi" [Nezâmi's view of women], *Iranshenasi* 5, 1 (Spring 1993): 105-10.

Shahidian, Hammed, "The Iranian Left and the `Woman Question' in the Revolution of 1978-9," *International Journal of Middle Eastern Studies* 26, 2 (May 1994): 223-47.

_____ "Doshvâri-hâ-ye negâresh-e târikh-e zanân dar Irân" [The problems of writing women's history in Iran], *Iran Nameh* 12, 1 (Winter 1994): 81-128.

Sprachman, Paul, "Review of Savushun: A Novel About Modern Iran," in *Iran Shenasi* 3, 1 (Spring 1991):194-9.

Tabari, Azar and Nahid Yeganeh, eds., *In the Shadow of Islam: The Women's Movement in Iran* (London: Zed Press, 1982).

Taraghi, Goli, "Surat-e azali-ye zan va zohur-e namâdin-e ân dar ash`âr-e Forugh-e Farrokhzâd" [Images of the archetypal mother/feminine in the poetry of Forugh Farrokhzad], *Iran Nameh* 7, 4 (Summer 1989): 657-73.

Vial, Charles, *Le personnage de la femme dans le roman et la nouvelle en Égypte de 1914 à 1960* (Damascus: Institut Français de Damas, 1979).

Women's Organization of Iran, *Ketâb-nâmeh-ye âsâr-e zanân-e Irân* [Statistics on Iranian women's publications] (Tehran: Sâzemân-e Zanân-e Irân, 1349/1970)

Yâvari, Hurâ, "Nâ-hamzamâni-ye dâstân va ensân" [Reflections on the influence of Gabriel García Márquez on 3 post-revolutionary Persian novels], *Iran Nameh* 9, 4 (Autumn 1991): 635-43.

_____ "Ta'amolli dar *Tubâ va ma`nâ-ye shab*, neveshteh-ye Shahrush-e Pârsipur" [Reflections on the novel *Tuba and the Meaning of Night*, by Shahrnush Parsipur], *Iran Nameh* 8, 1 (Winter 1990): 130-41.

Zavvâriân, Zahrâ, *Tasvir-e zan dar dah sâl-e dâstân-nevisi-ye enqelâb-e Eslâmi* [The image of women in fiction during the ten years since the Islamic Revolution] (Tehran: Howzeh-ye Honari-ye Sâzemân-e Tablighât-e Eslâmi, 1370/1991)

Zeidan, Joseph, *Arab Women Novelists: The Formative Years and Beyond* (Albany: State University of New York Press, 1995).

In A Voice Of Their Own

Goli Taraqqi [also spelled in English Taraghi] was born in 1939 in Tehran. Her father, Lotfollah Taraqqi, was the founder of the journals *Taraqqi (Progress)* and *Asiâ-ye javân (Young Asia)*, through which he supported the cause of modernization. Her mother, who was "elegant, pretty and sweet, but rather banal", was from a cultured family. Goli Taraqqi was sent to the United States in 1954 to pursue further education; she graduated from Drake University in 1960, with a B.A. in philosophy. She returned to Iran and worked at the Plan Organization - an Iranian government agency. She also taught philosophy and the interpretation of myths and symbols at Tehran University. In 1969, she published a collection of short stories entitled *I Too Am Che Guevara (Man ham Che Guevara hastam)*. In 1979, following the Islamic Revolution, she published a short story, which is considered one of her best, entitled *"The Great Lady of My Soul"* (*"Bozorg bânu-ye ruh-e man"*); this short story has been translated to English by Faridoun Farrokh and published twice (*Iranian Studies* 15.1-4 1982), and in *A Walnut Sapling on Masih's Grave and Other Stories by Iranian Women* (Heinemann, 1993). The French version of this story was awarded the 1985 Contre-Ciel Short Story Prize. Her 1973 novel *Khvâb-e zemestâni* has been translated into English (*Winter Sleep*, Mazda Publishers, 1994) and French (*Sommeil d'hiver*, Éditions Gallimard, 1986). She has been a contributor to numerous journals and has recently published a book entitled *Scattered Memories (Khâtereh-hâ-ye parâkandeh*, 2nd ed., 1994). She currently lives in Paris, France.

Taraqqi frequently delves into the inner emotional world of her characters through a stream of consciousness narrative technique. In this story, *"A House in the Heavens"* (*"Khâneh-'i dar âsemân"*) from *Khâtereh-hâ-ye parâkandeh* (Tehran: Bâgh-e Âyeneh, 1992, pp. 175-198), she explores the thoughts and feelings of an elderly Iranian woman and her sense of dislocation and alienation from home and family after fleeing from the war in Iran.

1

A House in the Heavens

Goli Taraqqi

It was a bad summer — hot, with no water and no electricity. There was a war on, and with it came fear and darkness. Masood D., like a man tossing in a nightmarish sleep, confused, giddy and distressed, took his wife and children by the hand and hastily left for Europe. Without thinking about it, without knowing what the future would bring. He didn't want to be wise, cautious and farsighted. He didn't want to consult with anyone — those who were more experienced, those who were afraid of dislocation and change, or those who believed in their homeland, their traditions and their roots, and had decided to stay home out of moral principle.

Masood D. hated war and was afraid of death. Nightly worries robbed him of his strength and peace, and painful anxieties tormented him at dawn. He had to go away. He had to run away and settle down in a safe place—somewhere far away from the commotion, bombs and explosions, far away from the possibility of death and madness. He made the arrangements secretly, quick as a flash. He put his furniture on sale and sold his house for almost nothing to the first customer. He got a visa, bought a ticket and packed his belongings. He was just about to leave when, like a man delirious with fever, his eyes fell upon his old mother and the ground under his feet caved in. He asked himself what would happen to her, and a wrenching pain shot through his innards with such force that he momentarily forgot about the war[1] and death and decided to stay.

All this time, Mahin-Banu had been watching, without questioning, objecting, or expressing herself in any way. She had seen them putting everything she owned up for sale and had not said a thing. She had seen strangers traipsing through the rooms of her house, and had not so much as opened her mouth. She had sat in a corner by the wall, on a big Tabrizi carpet—her ancestral keepsake—and with suppressed grief, stroked the velvet flowers and the colorful patterns of the rug, the last remaining artifact of the old days. The final contact of her fingertips with that old familiar object was reminiscent of how one might touch a lukewarm body in the last moments of its life. She had clutched at the fringe of the table cloth and held it in her grasp for a moment and her gaze had followed closely on the heels of the porcelain bowls as they were passed from hand to hand and of the tall Russian floor lamps, when they had been sold. She had wanted to say, "No! I won't give up the cashmere bundles or my wedding mirror," or to take something away and hide it. But she had said nothing. She was sitting in a corner, quiet and invisible, wounded in spirit, witnessing the departure of the clock, the table and chairs, the china and the gold-plated frames—all of them like an old mother's children setting off for foreign lands. She understood that hardship was awaiting her and accepted it. She did not reproach her son for it. She herself had registered the house in his name years before. They had agreed not to sell the house before her death. It was an old agreement, from the days before the Revolution and the war with Iraq, before terror and confusion had seized her children.

Mahin-Banu desired nothing but the health and well-being of her son, and of her daughter, who was married to an English man and was not living in Tehran. She would give up the rug beneath her feet—and she had done it, too—she would give her very life— which no one was after and was, in any case, coming to an end. Her children were in love with her, too. It would never have

---

[1]Referring to the Iran-Iraq War (1980-1988).

crossed Masood D.'s mind to abandon his mother and run away, or to leave her in the hands of God, homeless, possessionless and penniless, in order to save his own skin. But, in the distress and confusion, in the madness of war and bombing and imminent death, he had lost his wits and was no longer responsible for his actions or his instincts. Mahin-Banu realized all this and her silence, submission and resignation stemmed from this maternal wisdom. Of course, she had cried. She cried long and hard, secretly, when the others were not looking—at night in bed under the sheet, during the day in the bathroom with the door closed, behind the tall pine trees in the garden. She loved the cashmere, the rugs and the old objects, keepsakes of her father and her husband and a reminder of the happy days of her youth; she had grown old with them, and there was a timeless kinship between them. Her memories whirled about through the air, through the rooms of the house, like a thousand scattered images. The footprints and fingerprints of her childhood were etched in the stone-paved courtyard and on the brick walls. She knew no other place as her own outside this house, and she could see that this place was no longer hers, that no place belonged to her anymore. It was as if the ground under her feet had caved in and she was suspended in the air. Like a sick or dying cat, she wanted to slink off, head hung low, and just disappear.

But she could tell her health was good and that she was not about to die. Others had imposed old age on her, fixing her age with ruthless stares and their unfair estimates, flaunting the fact of the passing years in her face. She had a young image of herself, reflected in the mirrors of days gone by and the happy memories of old times. Her heart was beating and her eyes were open to the world around her. She was waiting for the future, for the arrival of spring and summer. She had a thousand hopes and wishes— for herself, her children, her grandchildren and their offspring. Seventy-four, seventy-six or was it more? Other people made such calculations, tried to figure the date of her marriage, of her birth; otherwise, Mahin-Banu never imagined herself a day over forty. She alone knew it, felt it and believed in it. But now, with no social standing and no place of her own, she no longer knew what era she had stumbled into, who she was, where, or what she should do. She had become a superfluous thing, having no place in the natural order of the cosmos, like a fallen star, exiled to a chaotic corner of the heavens. She wished it were not so. Death was in the distance, her feet sought the ground, her body sucked in the heat and particles of light, and her thoughts were bound by a thousand invisible threads to the sweet nooks and crannies of life.

It was agreed that Mahin-Banu would spend several weeks or more (perhaps two or three months) with her sister until Masood D. settled in Paris, found a house, a job and got his life in order. Then, at the proper time, with a light heart and a tranquil mind, he would send for his mother. Her daughter was also thinking about her. Despite her small income and the high cost of living, she was phoning regularly from London to invite her mother to come there. Her English son-in-law was a kind man, too, insisting to have his mother-in-law stay at their home. Only, they had to wait a while. Everything would eventually turn out fine, maybe even better than before. And Mahin-Banu was patient and wise, and her children were indebted to her inherent common sense.

The first two weeks went by rather hard; dislocation wasn't easy and Mahin-Banu wasn't used to sleeping in other people's homes. She was addicted to her room, her own bed and pillow, the bustle of the alley, the comings and goings of her old neighbors. She was even addicted to the old smell of the kitchen and the familiar musty odor of the stairs leading to the rooftop, and, of course, to the scent of honeysuckle by her window and to the tall and ever-present lombardy poplars, which were as old as her father. Her sister was kind and hospitable, and her brother-in-law, Dr. Yunes Khan, minded his own business. He was a dejected, lonely man, full of regret over being separated from his children, all seven of whom had left Iran after the Revolution. His oldest son had taken up residence in Australia, where seeing him would be impossible. His twin daughters—his favorites—were in the United States. His middle son was flitting about between Singapore, Thailand and Japan, and his youngest son was constantly on the move. One of his daughters (to the best of his recollection—he wasn't sure, his memory was unreliable) was a citizen of Canada, or India, or some unknown country in Africa.

His mother and her sister were close, and this gave Masood

some comfort; his conscience was at peace. He knew that his mother was comfortable, and this much was true. However, the nightly bombing and the damned missile attacks which followed had brought about drastic changes in the calm personality of Dr. Yunes Khan. He would get strange ideas and was suspicious about everybody for no reason. He would stand behind doors, eavesdropping; he would go through his wife's purse or search his sister-in-law's suitcase. He would hide his own worthless junk and forget where he had put it. He was sure that Mahin-Banu had taken his glasses and cigarette lighter. He would tell his wife, his wife would object and the couple would get into an argument about it. Mahin-Banu, listening to all this while crouching at her door, wanted to collapse in a heap of shame. She was beside herself, counting the days until it would be time, as soon as possible, to go to Europe and settle down somewhere with her children. She felt sorry for Dr. Yunes Khan, though, knowing that his behavior was not intentional or malicious. Even the day when her finger got caught in the door and her whole fingernail fell out, or the night when her brother-in-law messed up her bed and searched her pockets, looking for his agate ring, she did not groan, weep, object or complain. She said to herself that these were passing troubles, and she thanked God that her children were healthy and that she herself was alive and alert, despite all these incidents.

The promised day arrived at last. Mahin-Banu thought that she was dreaming and tears of joy were raining down—this from a person whose eyes did not easily cry in the presence of others! She couldn't help it. She kept kissing her grandchildren on the head and face and had no thought of sleep or rest, despite being on her feet all night—in the airport, in Customs, as they searched her baggage—despite her purse getting lost, despite leaving behind her spectacles and her medicine, despite her aching feet, her sudden dizzy spell and the damned nausea during the flight. Despite all this, if they had let her, she would have gone on talking all day and kissing the heads and faces of her grandchildren, her son and her daughter-in-law; she would have walked in that tiny apartment, no bigger than a mouse hole, and she would have asked, in her excitement and confusion, a thousand incomprehensible questions about this or that.

The first two nights, they firmly insisted that Mahin-Banu should sleep in the kids' room. For the kids they spread a mattress in the living room and softly whispered in their ears that Grandmother had just arrived and she was very tired—they should be kind to her. Later, they would move her bed to another room and the kids could have their own room back again.

Mahin-Banu saw the kids' frowning and pouting, and it made her unhappy. She wanted to say something, but was too embarrassed. She didn't have the energy either; her whole body was quaking with exhaustion. As soon as she laid her head on the pillow, she fell asleep. She slept like a log, but awoke with a start before dawn. She felt that an iron weight had been laid on her chest and a troublesome, unknown feeling—a kind of shame, or a sense of inferiority or guilt, almost a feeling of pain—coursed through her body. She remembered the vexed look of her grandchildren and she felt uneasy and upset about commandeering their room. She felt as though someone were poking her or had put needles in her mattress and in the pillow under her head. She would have preferred to sleep by the door in the hallway, or curl up in an armchair in the corner, than to take someone else's place. On the third day, they moved her and Mahin-Banu breathed a sigh of relief. They gave her a light foam-rubber mattress, which she spread out in the living room at night and hid under the couch during the day. They had put her suitcases in a corner of the kitchen and she carried her bag around with her from this room to that. The closets were so full of clothes that they wouldn't close properly and all sorts of things were stuffed under the beds. There was no room to move around. Mahin-Banu had lived her whole life in a house full of bright rooms with views of the sky, the sun, gardens and flower-beds. Her room had a closet and a wardrobe; hundreds of suitcases could be stored in the upstairs storeroom and a whole truck-load of things could be stored in the basement. Well, these were all history. Life has ups and downs, and sleeping in the corner of the living room was not all bad. Of course, there was too much noise in the alley, and the subway train would make the windows of the apartment shudder as it passed nearby. But from the very first, Mahin-Banu told herself that this was how people lived in Europe. There was no reason to complain. Thank

God that she was with her children and her life had a semblance of order.

Her grandchildren were happy with their lives, too. They loved their school and had made friends with a bunch of Arab and Portuguese classmates. From time to time, they would throw a party and Mahin-Banu had to sleep somewhere else. She would pick up her mattress and search out a quiet corner. But where? There were two bedrooms, a long narrow kitchen and a small bathroom with a toilet in the corner. She couldn't sleep in the bedroom of her son and daughter-in-law, though the former insisted and the latter had no complaint. There was no room in the kids' bedroom; there were two beds next to each other, a bunch of books, shoes, tennis rackets and a soccer ball on the floor. That left the kitchen. She wouldn't mind. How much space would Mahin-Banu take anyway? She was small as a child—skinny, delicate and fragile; she would fit anywhere, even in the closet or under the bed. She stretched out in the bathtub a couple of times, and she actually fell asleep there, but her son objected vociferously and made her sleep on his own bed beside his wife. That was Mahin-Banu's worst night. She was embarrassed in front of her daughter-in-law. She lay as far away as possible, right on the edge of the bed, such that if she moved, she would have fallen off the bed.

Her eyes remained half-open all night long. The sheet felt scratchy on her body and her skin crawled. She had curled herself up into a little ball: if you had pushed her, she would have rolled over and over until she got to the other end of the room. Her daughter-in-law tolerated the situation three or four nights. Then she kindly made her husband understand that to continue the arrangement would not be right. Although Masood D. was a quiet, sensible man, for no discernible reason he exploded all of a sudden. He shouted and everybody heard him. The kids were terrified and the husband and wife set at one another's throats, saying things they had never said before. Mahin-Banu nearly dropped dead of shame and called down curses on herself for having disturbed their family life. She decided that very day to leave. She packed her suitcase, she put on her jacket and shoes. She sat on the chair in the hallway and waited—waited for her heartbeat to subside and to collect her thoughts about where she could go. She would go back to Tehran. That was the best thing to do. She would go to her sister's house. Dr. Yunes Khan and his crazy behavior again? No! That was impossible. She would go to her cousin's house. She had forgotten that her cousin had passed away two months ago. Remembering now, she began to cry. She would go to her paternal cousin's house, or to her nephews' house (her nephews had gone to the United States). She would go to the graveyard, or to hell; she would go begging or serve as a maid. After all, she would be in her own country. She would lay her head down in the dirt and die, but she wouldn't stay here. No way.

Fortunately, Mahin-Banu's daughter, Manizheh (who was called Maggie in Europe), called from London and begged them to put her mother on an airplane and send her to her that very day, that very instant. It wasn't possible, of course, to send her that very minute, but they took her to the airport the following week. Like a bird released from its cage, Mahin-Banu's spirit soared. The plane was like a house—warm and secure. She had her seat, her very own seat. Her place was reserved and it could not be taken away from her. If it were possible to give her a seat on the ground—one square foot, a place which she could call her very own, that was all she asked for. She ate her meal with good appetite and thought of Naneh Khanoom, who used to bring in her dinner tray, back in those days when she used to be somebody and had social standing. How her heart had broken when she had heard that Naneh Khanoom's grandson was martyred in the war and her son had been taken to the mental hospital. If all that hadn't happened, things would have been different. Masood D. wanted to rent a small place for his mother and put her under Naneh Khanoom's care. This was the best solution for everyone, both for himself and for his mother. But who knows what will happen tomorrow? A mortar shell fell on the head of Naneh Khanoom's grandson and did him in on the spot. A few people came from Sabzevar and caused a great commotion. People came from the *Komiteh*, from the *Martyrs' Foundation*, expressing congratulations and condolences.[2] They took Naneh Khanoom back to her own village. She was given a room and a monthly pension. She agreed to stay there. All of this had happened before Mahin-Banu went to her sister's house.

Maggie (the former Manizheh) embraced her mother and hugged her so lovingly and nostalgically that Mahin-Banu let out a sigh of both pain and joy. Her son-in-law also kissed her and vigorously shook her hand. David Oakley was a good man. He had Jewish blood and that explained his warmth. Mahin-Banu didn't like her daughter to be married to an English Jew. She would have liked to have an Iranian Muslim for a son-in-law. But she hadn't said a thing; she did not interfere in her children's affairs. Nonetheless, there was a sadness in the recesses of her heart until the day when she saw David Oakley's healthy face and sincere, open eyes, at which point a heavy weight was lifted from her chest. She slipped her arm in the crook of his masculine arm and laughed. The contrast made her realize just how skinny and small she was—she didn't even reach her son-in-law's waist. She was like a little chick. She weighed no more than forty kilos, perhaps even less, with hollow bones and legs as thin as pencils.

It was rainy and cold. David Oakley had a car. He put the suitcases in the trunk of his car and gave a firm joyful pat on Mahin-Banu's delicate shoulder. Maggie sat beside her mother and laid her head on her aching shoulder. She whispered in her ear that she would no longer let her go back to Paris or Tehran. All this tender affection made Mahin-Banu's heart throb. She closed her eyes and fell asleep, but didn't dream.

Maggie and David Oakley's apartment was on the fourth floor, with no elevator. Mahin-Banu was exhausted and sleepy-headed. She was feeling dizzy. David Oakley picked up his mother-in-law, who was as light as a blade of straw. Mahin-Banu screamed, stiff-

---

[2] The Iranian government referred to soldiers and citizens killed in the War as "martyrs", and notified the next-of-kin with the phrase "congratulations and condolences"—that is condolences for your loss, but congratulations that your loved one has become a martyr, served his country and gone to heaven.

ened her body like a pencil and stayed in that position. Maggie laughed. David Oakley was in a good mood, too. He was holding his mother-in-law under his arm like a wooden doll and climbing the stairs. Mahin-Banu didn't even blink. She couldn't believe it; she didn't know whether she should laugh, scream or cry. Until that moment, nothing like this had ever happened to her. She wasn't able to react naturally or show her approval or disapproval of what was happening to her. She felt that she wasn't herself— she had turned into an object, a broom or a chair, which had been bought at the market. Being a broom was a new experience, with its own peculiar world.

*****

Maggie's apartment was smaller than her brother's. It had only one bedroom. But they had no children. They did have a dog, big and hairy, as tall as Mahin-Banu. David Oakley was a rational and logical man. His actions were regular and calculated. He didn't get emotional; he thought. He was straightforward and didn't stand on ceremony. They agreed that Mahin-Banu would sleep on the couch in the living room. Whenever the couple were entertaining, she would go to sleep on the bed in their bedroom and wait there half-asleep, until the guests left. Of course, it wasn't a solution according to everyone's desire, but what else could be done? Mahin Banu didn't say anything. She never did. Even if she had had something to say, she knew that it wasn't the time to say it, and this made life easier for everyone.

David Oakley was a teacher. He taught Economics and painstakingly noted down every household expense. Fortunately, Mahin-Banu was only as big as a little chick and she tried to eat even less food than a household sparrow. Maggie was going to school. She was studying accounting. The couple would leave in the morning and return at night, exhausted. They did not even have the energy to talk, and even when they did, they would only talk about high prices and the cost of living. Mahin-Banu had no money of her own. On her very first day there, she had begged and pleaded with her daughter to take her gold bracelet and ruby earrings and sell them. Maggie had said, "No way!" Her husband had said, "No problem!" Maggie had cried and said, "No!," but later she had accepted them, reluctantly of course, in accordance with her husband's advice.

Mahin-Banu had learned to talk to herself. She couldn't understand her son-in-law's language and Maggie was obliged to talk to her husband in English or not to talk at all. They ate their evening meals in silence. Maggie would do her homework and David Oakley would read the paper, every page, cover to cover. Then, all three of them would watch T.V.: programs about science or culture, discussions or interviews. Mahin-Banu would stare at the T.V. screen, but she saw nothing and understand nothing. She would plunge into a sea of memories, into a different place and time. And during the day she was all alone. She would clean and tidy up the apartment, arrange the flowers in the vase on the windowsill and look out on the endless rain and dark city skies. She was afraid of David Oakley's dog, too, and most days stayed in the bedroom until her daughter would come home. From time to time she would go out, weather permitting. She would sit in the park across from the apartment and shiver. It was a harsh winter and she caught a cold. First her throat swelled up, then it spread into her chest. What a cough! It felt like all her insides would come right out her mouth. To complicate matters, the noise of her coughing kept the next-door neighbor awake. He would pound on the wall with his fist, and Mahin-Banu would stick her head under the pillow. She would stuff the corner of the sheet into her mouth to inhale.

With the arrival of the spring, everything changed. A few sunbeams appeared from behind the clouds and people acted lighthearted. David Oakley took three days off work and took his wife and mother-in-law sightseeing. They all had a good time. Maggie bought pills and other medicines to help her mother regain her strength. Mahin-Banu gained a couple of kilos and thanked God from the bottom of her heart. But no sooner had she finished giving thanks than things took a turn for the worse. It was the beginning of the summer. David Oakley was going to go to the mountains for two months to stay with his aunt. It was impossible to take Mahin-Banu with them. They were going to sublet the apartment in these two months to help out with the expenses. It was understandable, especially since their mother-in-law's expenses had been added to theirs, and they had to make it up somehow. They agreed to send Mahin-Banu back to her son in Paris. The decision was made quickly. They put her on a plane without even consulting Masood D. and told him that his mother was on her way. It was bad timing. Although Masood D. was happy to see his mother once again and visit with her, he couldn't take her on at that particular time. Any other time she would have been welcomed with open arms, mind you. He said it wouldn't work out. It's summertime and they were all going to the south of France. They didn't have enough money for a hotel or a beach-house; they would sleep in a tent, on the beach or out in the desert, well not the desert, but in a forest or a field. Wherever they went, in any case, to take Mahin-Banu with them was out of the question. The sister and brother argued. David Oakley came up with several solutions. They all put their minds together and decided to send Mahin-Banu back to London and make arrangements for her to stay there.

Mahin-Banu overheard their discussions, though they talked with hushed voices and tried to whisper into the phone. With the tip of her toes, she would press into the ground beneath her feet, hoping that a hole would open up and swallow her. She understood that she was being passed from hand to hand like excess baggage, and it had made her dizzy.

Firoozeh Khanoom was one of Maggie's close friends. She owned a dry cleaning shop and made her living by it. They asked her for help. Firoozeh Khanoom was good-looking and witty. She said that she herself was living in a small room and had no room for a guest, but that there was an empty storage-room in the back of the dry cleaning shop. It didn't have any window, but it was warm and safe. David Oakley agreed. Maggie felt uneasy about it, but she had no other option and didn't say anything. Mahin-Banu agreed, too. She just longed to settle the matter as soon as possible.

The room behind the dry cleaning shop was damp and dimly-lit. The first night, Mahin-Banu cried until dawn and begged God to help her die. She wondered what had made her hold on life so firm, and where her strength came from. She saw that her strength grew out of her love for her children and so she vowed to empty her heart of this love so that she could die in peace.

Firoozeh Khanoom was an amiable woman, worth more than ten men. She had a husband, too, who lived in Tehran—one of those mournful, opium-addicted husbands. He came to Europe once a year, at his wife's expense. He would moan and groan, complaining about absolutely everything. He was a depressed, useless, scarecrow of a man. In the past he had been somebody, or at least he imagined he had been. He was an educated man, well-read, a translator. But life's first blow had knocked him out, dazed and despairing. Firoozeh Khanoom was a lion of a woman; she had no patience for moaning and groaning. She sent her children off to England. She herself got up and followed, opened up a business. She was generous and gracious, too. She would help those around her—those who deserved to be helped. When she saw Mahin-Banu, with that sweet face and those sad honey-colored eyes, she was charmed by her. She shopped for her and looked after her. She would seat her in the dry cleaning shop by the machines and read Persian books and newspapers to amuse her.

Karim Khan, Mahin-Banu's brother, lived in Canada. He had money and a house. It even had a small garden with a few birds and a rabbit. Through an acquaintance, he heard a greatly embellished story about his sister's unsuitable situation and raised a great fuss. It offended him so much that he wrote a letter to his niece and nephew, insulting and belittling them (perhaps he went a bit too far, but he couldn't control himself). He ordered them to make arrangements for his sister. He had an acquaintance at the Canadian Embassy through whom he got Mahin-Banu a visa and sent her a plane ticket. As soon as Masood D. or Maggie tried to butt in, he phoned and yelled at both of them. Since he was the oldest member of the family, they all gave in.

It was the beginning of winter when Mahin-Banu set out for Canada. She was happy to be between heaven and earth once again. This was the longest distance she had gone, and how wonderful it was! She sat by the window, her eyes fixed upon the pure, bright light outside. Her seat was warm and soft. Exactly what she wanted: a little space that others could not violate. She had a fever, and the sunshine from the window was just the thing. She kept dozing off momentarily, and her head falling onto her chest would wake her up again. Her eyelids would open halfway and she would gaze out toward the edge of the horizon, the great expanse, spread out endlessly. Beneath her feet was a field of white clouds, bright, clean, light, like a heavenly dream, a comforting dream of the angels nigh unto God.

Somebody whispered in her ear—the passenger sitting next to her. She didn't hear. She didn't want her food-tray and turned the other way. She pressed her face against the windowpane and soaked up the sunshine with her bewitched eyes. She felt a thousand tiny stars twinkling between the layers of her thoughts, lighting a lamp within her.

The entire sky above was blue, with not a wisp of cloud, with not a rude bump or jarring jolt, extending out beyond the boundaries of the imagination, to the beginning of everything, beyond the pale of this world's shapes and conventions. Mahin-Banu saw herself as a twelve year-old girl, busy playing in the garden at *Damavand*. It was snowing, and her finger tips were numb from touching the hollow, frozen flakes. She watched the dazzling snowfall in the grey distance of the horizon and it seemed to her that her feet were uprooted from the earth, and she was flying heavenward through the sky. She loved this game; even when she had grown old, she never forgot this game. She would sit by the window and Naneh Khanoom would bring her tea and rock-candy. Like two people possessed by jinn, the both of them would sit there staring at the unbroken whiteness of the snow outside and gradually fall asleep. She would wake up in the middle of the night, knowing that it was still snowing, and listen. The whole city was asleep, petrified, under a white cover, like a house with nobody in it, its furniture hidden under clean sheets. Not a sound could be heard, except the magical silence of the void, overflowing with nothing, with the silent presence of God.

Throughout the journey, Mahin-Banu, feverish and wet with perspiration, yet cheerful, sat by the window, so mesmerized and enchanted by the view that she no longer remembered where she was or who. She kept dreaming and waking up. She kept looking. She kept remembering the past, kept going back. She would spin round and round. She was in the snow, in the middle of the sky. She was playing on the slide, on the swing. She was everywhere, all at once. She saw fluttering through space, or all lined up in the air, a thousand images of Mahin-Banu at different ages—an old woman, a child, a youth, in this life and in other eras of history. One woman to the power of infinity, linked together as if in an eternal chain. It was the first time that Mahin-Banu had not thought about her children and the people on the earth, about her large carpet and the cashmere, about her house on Pahlavi Avenue and her earthly memories.

She was above the clouds, and the vast expanse was slowly permeating through her body, settling at the bottom of her soul. Like the pleasant warmth of autumn, soft and moist, it wove a cocoon around her, spun a web, opened a parasol above her head. It was as if she was in the belly of the world, secure and immune, beyond time.

Karim Khan was waiting impatiently for his sister's arrival. He had decided to have her live with him and was ashamed of the thoughtlessness of his niece and nephew. He began crying as soon as his eyes fell upon Mahin-Banu. He himself was lonesome and separated by great distances from his relatives. He longed for home a thousand times a day, but would talk himself out of it. Seeing his sister—old, broken and homeless—renewed his sense of searing loss. He said to himself, "To hell with life far away from home!," and, for just a moment, the idea of going back took hold of him. He owned property and a garden; he would return to his house and live together with Mahin-Banu. They were very close— they were about the same age and had grown up together. When he saw Mahin-Banu, he was alarmed. How gaunt, pale and disoriented she was! She did not seem to see what she was looking at and she was absent-minded. When he took her hand, he was shocked—she was nothing but a warm skeleton! He spoke to her, she wouldn't hear, she wouldn't understand. Her responses had nothing to do with the subject at hand. Shocked and disturbed, Karim Khan embraced his sister and kissed her on the head and face. He felt the full weight of his years and a painful twinge shot through his heart.

When they reached home, he had Mahin-Banu lie down on a

huge bed and called the doctor. He called Mahin-Banu's children
and told them about their mother's condition. He explained to
them that it was exhaustion, lack of sleep and high blood pressure;
it was nothing serious, nothing to worry about. He began tending
to his sister. He was excited and disconcerted and had so much to
tell her that he didn't know where to begin. He reminisced about
the past, their childhood days, all the yesterdays and the days before that. He told her about himself and his sudden decision to
return home. He laughed and was happy. He couldn't believe
that he had decided to go back home; he was indebted to his sister
for this sudden happiness. He himself didn't know how he had
arrived at this notion. Perhaps seeing his sister's blank expression
and the air of displacement she had about her moved him.

He looked in Mahin-Banu's blank eyes, which appeared
drained of all familiar memories or logical thoughts, and it gave
him a scare. He saw the traces of homesickness in her and a shudder crept through the depth of his being. It suddenly dawned on
him just how forlorn and lonely he was, how the ground under his
feet was hollow, how, like a traveller in a strange land, passing
through a sad, cold train station, his existence was temporary and
fleeting.

He held Mahin-Banu's hand and kissed it. He told her that her
days of wandering homeless from door to door were over. As
soon as she got better, they would go back home, to Iran. Mahin-
Banu closed her eyes and saw herself sitting at the window of the
airplane. The blue expanse was calling to her. She fell asleep and
dreamed of the sky once more, flowing like a rolling sea towards
the bright open plains of existence.

She didn't know how many days she had been asleep. She was
thirsty. She got up. Her knees trembled. Karim Khan wasn't at
home. She looked around. She couldn't remember where she was.
A dim light was coming through the lacy curtain. She went closer
and grabbed the edge of the chair. She stood there to catch her
breath. She took two steps forward and felt as though she had
moved a whole mountain. Sweat poured off her head and face.
She pulled aside the curtain with her trembling hand. It was
snowing. She listened: that same old inviting silence. Naneh
Khanoom had brought her tea and rock-sugar. She had stood by

the door, weeping. Her grandson had been martyred. She was going to Sabzevar. Mahin-Banu said, "Naneh Khanoom, wait! Let me give you some money, you'll need it for the journey," and she put her hand on the doorknob. She was tired and longed to sit down. She was looking for her seat; the stewardess was looking at her ticket. A cold breeze struck her in the face. She shivered. It was snowing—heavy snowflakes, as big as saucers. She went on a little further. Her foot slid. It was cold inside the plane. She couldn't find her seat. She went a little further ahead.

A white road lay stretched out before her feet. The snow was getting in her eyes. Mt. Damavand, tall and solid, majestic, was looking down on her from afar. It was as magnificent as her father when he used to stand up to say his prayers and the wind would blow under his *aba*. His head had seemed to reach the sky and his feet to be rooted in the ground. How good it was when she had lived in the shade of such a mountain, whose summit reached the sky, a mountain magical and awe-inspiring—this man, who stood between the two marble columns of the veranda at the noonday prayer, his shadow extending to the ends of the earth. What pleasure it used to bring, crawling under his *aba* or climbing up on his shoulders, on to the world's tallest peak, above and beyond the earth, and its tiny mudbrick houses and the people, small as ants, lowly and of no account. Looking through the plane's window, it was the same scene she saw—as though she were perched on her father's shoulders where no hand could touch her. Not her mother's scolding, reprimanding hands; not those of her bad-tempered teacher of religious law and jurisprudence, who was always talking about sin and repentance; not those of the neighborhood policeman, which would box her ears; not her husband, who would confine and subdue her; nor her children, who clung to her, eating her flesh and blood with beastly pleasure; not the hand of others, who established ethical standards and historical philosophies, filling her head with a crushing weight of words and circumscribing the horizons of her vision and the boundaries of her emotions with their little geometric rulers and their miserable arithmetic measures.

Somebody was calling her. Maybe it was coming from the other side of Mt. Damavand. She ran forward, turned around and then went left down a snow-filled street. She was hot, burning. She took off her jacket, unbuttoned her shirt and held her face towards the sky. She remembered her childhood game and laughed. The snow went in her mouth; it was delicious. She looked, and looked and looked, staring without blinking once. Her feet were uprooted from the earth. The snowflakes hung in the sky, as if nailed in place, while she went up and up. She was in the sky, above the clouds. She saw Mt. Damavand under her feet. Sitting on its summit, there was a big easy-chair, made of walnut and red velvet—the same chair that was in her father's study. The stewardess showed her the seat, which was especially reserved for her. She sat down. She was small as a child and was lost in the big chair. She wrapped her father's *aba* around herself and pressed her face against the windowpane. The sky was entirely blue, clear as a fountain of light, and the vast expanse—open, generous and magnanimous—was looking at her. She listened; there was no sound except the soft falling snow and death's sweet silence.

*****

Masood D. put the blame on his sister and held her responsible. His sister complained about Uncle Karim. David Oakley said such things often happen. Since he was teaching at the university, he referred to the law of cause and effect and the principles of history and economics. Firoozeh Khanoom felt sorry and then forgot. Others tried hard not to forget the story of Mahin-Banu, but they did. With all their hassles, hard luck, work and exhaustion; with the war going on and living life far away from home, was it even possible to remember and reflect? And Mahin-Banu understood this only too well. Thank God that she was a sensible woman.

Paris - October 15, 1991

Mihan Bahrâmi was born in Tehran and graduated from Tehran University. She studied psychology and the sociology of art at UCLA, but did not complete her degree. She is a movie critic, an accomplished painter and a fiction writer. She published a collection of short stories entitled *Animal: Seven Talks and a Story* (*Hayvân: Haft goftâr va yek qesseh*) in 1985. In 1990, she published another book entitled *The Seeker (Jostejugar)*. She lives in Tehran and is a contributor to the series *Ketâb-i Tehrân*, a collection of scholary and literary articles, poetry, short stories and book reviews.

This story, *"The Garden of Sorrow"* (*"Bâgh-e gham"*) from the collection *Hayvân* (Tehran: Enteshârât-e Damâvand, 1985, pp. 23-44), illustrates the complexities of one mother-daughter relationship in Iran, and the adjustments in family relationships brought on by remarriage.

2

The Garden of Sorrow
Mihan Bahrami

Our lane was narrow and the cob walls of the houses had a drab rural look about them. At the bend in the middle of the lane, a thick acacia leaned over the stream, gazing at the tips of its own branches. At the end of the lane stood our house, and just a little beyond it the lane dead-ended in a large, wide, wooden gate. Through the cracks between the planks, hammered into place with pegs, a large garden could be seen. The people of the neighborhood called it "Lane's End Garden."

Every day the neighbor kids and I would play tip-cat, jacks and jump rope. But as soon as the games were over and my playmates were on their way home, I would climb up the stairs in the court-yard of our house, which were flush with the garden wall, on to our roof and secretly gaze on the garden.

The garden was square and quite large. A narrow cobblestone path led from the gate, after which came neatly arranged vegetable patches, bordered by a row of bluish cabbage plants. In the square plots between the vegetable patches they planted chamomile and coriander. The white chamomile blossoms and the dark blue wild lilies looked like so many breeze-scattered petals floating gently on a surface of water. Further along, up past the vegetable patches, was a line of white and lombardy poplars. The silence of the garden was broken only by the cawing of the crows nesting in these trees and the sound of the bells of the pack animals bringing manure at noon. Then, the monotonous chirping of the crickets in the coriander bushes would mingle with the clank of the latten bells of pack animals to create a happy and hypnotic music; particularly on spring afternoons, it would make me giddy and the hot cob plaster of the rooftop would burn my toes. On such days I would not climb downstairs until they yelled at me or threatened me. The garden looked much more beautiful at noon than any other time. The gardeners would leave for lunch and the sparrows would swarm in the trees, their noisy chirping raising a ruckus.

Thousands of bright twinkling stars would sparkle in the lingering dew on the tips of plant sprouts and the trees and flowers would fall sleep under the soft umbrella of the song of crickets and beetles.

The trees of the garden knew me well; I had divided them into families. By the gate, there was a very old and thick plane tree, the grandfather of all the trees. Next, in the row of lombardy poplars, there was a family with three children: the two tall, thin trees that shook easily were the sons and the short tree with branches spread upward like an umbrella was their daughter. There were a few elm trees in the eastern corner of the garden—dark green and all of them single, without a mate. They reminded me of the spinster who lived a few houses down from ours and quarreled with everyone except the kids.

I was so attached to the trees, the vegetable patches, and the sound of the pack animals' bells that I would sense even the slightest of changes in them. If I closed my eyes, I could see them lifelike in my imagination, wavy and green as they actually were. And if I heard the sound of the bells, I would know whether the donkey carts were loaded or empty, whether they were coming or going. If I did not go to the rooftop every day, I would feel something was missing. I believed that an unknown being was waiting for me in the garden, and this was not just my imagination, because whenever I had my fill of the garden and started to go downstairs, my gaze would be drawn involuntarily to the west corner. There was a berry tree there, big and dark in color, which looked as if it had grown out of the top of a hill. The ground around the tree was piled with smashed leaves, garbage and patted dung, heaped half-way up the tree's trunk. Down the hill, across from the berry tree, the two dark hollow eyes of the window of an old door, which was always kept closed, were staring at me.

They called this place "the Snake Stable." My Granma used to say, "The landlord's snake's in the stable. Some while ago, the snake bit all the cows and donkeys tied up in the stable, and the old venom of the snake has turned their old hides to ash."

The gardener, Bemoon Ali, used to say, "The snake's an infidel. To kill a snake, whether it's infidel or Muslim, brings bad luck. That's why they've abandoned the stable." Some of the women used to say that they had seen the snake in the summer afternoons, dragging its wide, spotted body over the damp soil under the berry tree, its forked red tongue hanging out, panting, as it searched for water. Its mouth was so big that a small head could fit in it. The old gardeners used to say, "It's no snake any more; it's become a venomous serpent. If it comes close, it can kill with its venomous breath."

It was because of all these stories I'd heard that I would stare into the pane-less windows of that old door with mordant curiosity, in search of all the frightening thoughts that I could summon up at that moment. I was scared of the stable and the snake in it, but I was likewise attracted to it. Even as I watched the garden, I tried to keep my attention on the butterflies and the trees, or on Bemoon Ali's russet goat which was tied under the jujube tree. But a peculiar curiosity would draw my attention to the berry tree, and I would gaze into the blackness of the stable windows. After staring into the darkness for a while, I could see vague figures. Nonetheless, watching the garden was so enchanting for me that it occupied most of the hours I was alone, from the forenoon to the afternoon.

Evenings, however, were something else. We would spread throw-rugs on the rooftop by the wall, sprinkle the Rashti straw mats with water to soften them, bring the samovar up on the roof and stretch out under our bedrolls. On the other side, opposite the garden, past the cob-plastered arched rooftops and the Shah Abbasi caravansary, there were a large number of pine trees near an old house. Behind the branches of these pine trees, the glittering dome and the mosaic minarets of the Shahzadeh Shrine were visible. Beyond the dome and minarets, in the violet and blue horizon, under a big star which used to appear in the sky sooner than the others, there was a pitched-roof brick house with a long-legged stork standing on top. I never saw this bird put both its legs down at once.

From up there we could hear the jumbled noises of the streets and lanes, which would gradually fade away after sunset into the silence of the night and the mingled sounds of insects. Then the clock in the Shahzadeh Shrine would strike and the sound would echo off the branches of the pine trees and the multicolored tiles of the mosaic minarets. Right afterwards the melancholic bass voice of the muezzin would call out. What wonderful evenings! You could hear the bubbling of Granma's hookah and the reproachful tone of her voice as she would say her prayers and take the opportunity to ask forgiveness for her sins. I could see her doleful face from the rooftop or anywhere esle I would play. In answer to the neighbors who would say, "Grief will soon make you old and infirm," she would nod and while removing the lid of her hookah, she would wipe away the teardrops from the corners of her eyes with the edge of her kerchief.

How much I longed to grieve like her, pray like her, or mutter like her. But I did not like to smoke the hookah. I did like to sit and watch the crystal urn of water in her hookah. She used to drop a few petals of red or Damascus rose in it. Two dark wooden dolls, swollen with the hot moisture of the hookah, were attached to the tube passing through the urn. When she puffed, the dolls would spin amongst the bubbles as if they were chasing the rose leaves. I would laugh hysterically seeing them somersault in the water. Sometimes, however, when there wasn't much water in the urn, a wisp of smoke would snake out of the tube inside the urn on the surface of the water and the wooden dolls would remain fixed and motionless, and I would see the demon of Granma's stories, eddying down the tube to find the wooden dolls and swallow them up whole. I thought if Granma separated the top part of the hookah from the urn, the demon would escape into the room. Then, I would look at Granma whose face was tired and sad and I would think I should be like her. I wanted so very much to know how to grieve. I would purse my lips, sigh and swallow my saliva. Sometimes I would squeeze my throat to keep my saliva from going down easily and would try to burst into tears and show Granma that I could grieve like her. But, when she would take the hookah away, I would forget all about it and begin doing somersaults, gazing at the dome and minarets upside down. Sometimes I would recite the poem, written on the occasion of *Naser al-Din Shah's* death, which I had learned from my Granma:

> Naser al-Din, the Shah, the Just—
> The Grand Vazir and Head of State—
> set out one Friday for the Shrine.
>
> His harem ladies each and all
> were from house and home turned out.
> His harem children, every one,
> were into orphans turned.
>
> Turned out.....turned into....turned out.....

With each refrain of the poem, I would clap my hands once and touch my knees. I remember that I used to mispronounce the word 'Grand Vazir' as "grains of tare," and paid no attention to the meaning of the poems, no attention to anything. I just wanted to recite the poems and somersault, for it gave me pleasure. When I was completely exhausted, I would lie down on the mattress and watch the sky. The cool canvas bed-sheet smelled of humidity and cob plaster and the smell would make my body rubbery and weak. In the distance thousands of stars twinkled, and above my head, I could see "the Meccan Road," as the Milky Way was colloquially called. I used to think my father had taken the same road to go on his journey.

In the middle of the night when I would waken to the noise of fighting alley cats and the stifled lovemaking of nearby husbands and wives, the bright orb of the moon would move in tandem with a big star in the deep transparent sea of the night. A scary tuft of cloud in the shape of an open mouth would creep after them. The face of the moon was sad and the sun's fingerprints were visible on its cheek.

Come daytime, I was in a different world, leaping, jumping, playing in front of the gate of "Lane's End Garden." I would draw squares on the ground with a piece of charcoal to play tip-cat. All our time was spent playing hopscotch and giving piggy-back rides to the winners. How the neighbors—believing that black lines bring bad luck—would scold us as they wiped away the charcoal streaks with the tips of their feet. All for want of a piece of chalk.

*****

That morning, it was my turn to play. Hopping on one foot and pushing the stone across the lines, I saw Granma come out of the courtyard. Although my attention was focussed on the movement of the stone and the lines of the squares, Granma's tall though slightly bent frame caught my eye because she was wearing her formal dress—a white polka-dotted chador, black socks and Russian galoshes with red lining. She had tied the ends of her kerchief in order to keep them from covering her face. When she left our lane she would veil her face, but she was not bashful in front of the neighbors. Granma didn't see me and walked on by, but stopped to return the greetings of one of the neighbor women.   Granma exchanged pleasantries with her and then I heard Granma say: "Yes, my child! I said to myself I'm going to shed tears on his grave this Thursday night to lift this load off myself. I can't do it at home..." The neighbor woman said in a reproving voice, "What's the use? It's not gonna bring him back. Whatever you do, you should do it for her." And I noticed that she pointed at me. Granma said goodbye to her and left without looking at me. The neighbor woman grumbled, "After all this time she still feels his loss like it happened yesterday. God give her patience! I've never seen anybody mourn so for a son-in-law."

At that moment I could not fully comprehend the meaning of these words, but everything I had seen made me feel strange and perhaps for the first time I thought seriously about my father. For a moment I was lost in the distance, but the neighbor children's yelling brought me back to myself. They were picking up the stone at my feet and shouting, "You blew it in the fourth square! You gotta give four piggyback rides!   Fourth square..." For a while I stood there dumbfounded. "So, my father hasn't gone on a journey. He's dead, and now I'm an orphan." I looked at my playmates. "Did they know about this?"

I was overcome with terror. I don't know why I was so frightened. I had never considered myself an orphan because every orphan I had ever seen was clothed in rags like a beggar. To me, being an orphan meant being a beggar—like the kid who would stretch his hand out to us and say, "Have mercy on me—an orphan."

Among our playmates, there was a boy whose father had fallen in a well and drowned; the kid had big blue lesions from Oriental Sore under his eyes and snot from his runny nose was always congealed at one corner of his lips. It was disgusting. I did not want to have the slightest resemblance to him. In my eyes, he was a defective creature, and I used to torment him quite alot.

I liked myself very much. I was a pretty girl, everyone said so. My new shoes and my pretty dress seemed the best things in the world to me. I used to think at night that up in the sky, at the top of the sky, in a place with a golden dome decorated with mirrors like the Shahzadeh Shrine, sat a God who could see me. He was mindful of me and loved me and would return my father to me.

Perhaps I had not heard the neighbor's words correctly? Maybe my father had gone to Karbala? Maybe the neighbor woman wasn't pointing at me? I wanted to jump and play and forget about everything, but I couldn't. My legs felt heavy and I no longer wanted to see the neighbor kids.

I thought about Karbala. This was the first time that Karbala had become so important—even frightening—to me. I began to feel that I hated it. "Is Karbala some kind of place that whoever goes there doesn't come back?

What journey? No, I was sure that my father would come back. However, a part of my heart grew empty. Granma didn't seem the same to me as before. Her lie had put a distance between us. I could not listen to her the way I used to. Once again I remembered the neighbor woman saying, "He's not coming back again." I could not admit that my father, even if he was dead, would not come back again. I consoled myself with the thought that Granma, my mother and the others had not lied to me; so many people could not be lying. My father had gone on a journey. But I did not want him to have gone to Karbala. Some other city would be better; perhaps I had heard it wrong. Yet I would ask myself, "Then, where is he?" I did not dare ask Granma—I was afraid she would say he's gone to Karbala or that he's dead, both of which meant the same to me.

I stopped playing and went home. I was wondering whether I should grieve over my father's death or over his journey to a destination unknown to me. I sat opposite Granma and sighed. I tried to remain silent for a while like her and gently sway the upper half of my body, but the wooden dolls in the urn of water of her hookah were once again faced with some smoke coming down the tube, and concern for their situation distracted me.

*****

The summer went by and in the fall I went back to live with my mother. I was her only child. To me she was not just my mother or a beautiful creature: she was a fairy, the prince's girl with forty braids of hair from a fairy tale. I loved my mother more than anything else in the world. It was because of her that I had not noticed the absence of my father. Although she was kind of strict and sometimes impatient and ill-humored, her white luminous beauty used to make me proud in front of other children. No other child had a mother as beautiful as mine.

Those nights when we were alone she would tell me stories. Her warm and familiar tone of voice made everything she said seem real and true-to-life for me. Sometimes she would cut out paper dolls for me, folding them together and then opening them to lay them all out in a circle on a flat tray. Then, she would gently tap out a tune on the underside of the tray and I would laugh to see the paper dolls dance. Once in a while she would place the dolls in front of the wall, their backs to the lamp, and pull them with a string. Their shadows on the wall would make a little movie for me. She called these paper dolls the "Dasteh Aloo Dolls." These dolls were so real and dear to me that I would cry when one of them was torn. In the mornings I would never go to see them; the way they were scattered all over the tray would upset me. At night, however, in the light of the brass lamp, I would believe them; they would look alive to me.

*****

That fall when I returned from Granma's house, I noticed a change. My mother spent less time alone with me. There were many people coming and going. My aunts kept dropping by. Sometimes I would stop and listen to what they said. I did not know why they were talking about a person who was not there and whom I did not know. It seemed a guest was going to come. They were always talking about him, but it didn't make me worry. I was sure about my mother and our humble lives together, nothing in the world but that could worry me. Eventually, my mother seemed to be happier and more cheerful than before. She paid more attention to her appearance, she would shop and sew for herself, and sometimes she would hum a song when she was alone. This song was not like the ones she used to sing before, when she would lull me to sleep. Her lullabies were so beautiful that even when I was big I used to ask her to sing me lullabies. On long dark winter nights, under the warm *korsi* and white sheets, she would sing to me:

> Lullaby, my pennyroyal blossom, lullaby
> My child has come into the house
>
> Lullaby, my red rose, lullaby
> My child has come like a houri of paradise
>
> Lullaby my pistachio blossom, lullaby
> My child has come like a bouquet of flowers

But these days she would modulate her voice, reciting the words eloquently and I felt she wanted to believe what she was singing. Yet every time I approached her, her voice would tremble as if she were plagued by doubt. I liked her singing, even when she wasn't singing me a lullaby, but was singing for herself. A strange, but not sad, feeling would bring tears to my eyes. I would hide my head under the covers and hold my breath so that she wouldn't notice I was crying and stop singing.

*****

During those days I gradually grew nervous, like an animal before an earthquake strikes. I did not know why. I wondered if my mother had seen me eating jam from the jar or snatching her change from under the rug, or perhaps she had discovered the broken pieces of the plate that I had hidden in the colander and knew that I had done it. I would approach her cautiously and never fuss. I did not ask her constantly to tell me stories at night. I had promised myself to be a good girl. One day, during the call to evening prayer, I vowed that if my father returned from his journey or if my mother would act the way she used to, I would no longer blow out the candles at the public drinking-place, which was opposite our house, and would not make waxen dolls out of the half-burned candles. I even promised to light candles there on Thursday nights and to give my pocket-money to that orphan kid with the Oriental Sore under his eyes I used to torment. I promised that I would no longer swing from the chain of the drinking-cup at the public drinking-place, and that I would pick up the small pieces of bread dropped in the alley and kiss them and put them on the ledge by the wall so no one would step on them. I even decided to learn how to say the ritual prayers from Granma.

One day our house was in commotion: the rooms were cleaned, chairs were set. In the corner room, the one with the solid foundation, they spread a white tablecloth on the rug. At the head of the tablecloth, they placed a full-size mirror that was a keepsake from my mother's first marriage and, in the past, used to stand next to a framed picture of my father. They lit the two lamps with the brass bases and blue semi-vitrified porcelain shades, on which were painted pictures of a peacock. They dressed me in my shiny velvet dress and told me to keep out of the way.

I went to the corner room on the other side of the yard. They had set the framed picture of my father, which had always hung on the wall of the reception room, on the mantle in this room. My mother was there standing by the mirror plucking her eyebrows with a pair of ivory-handled tweezers. A swollen red crescent had risen above her bright honey-colored eyes. I stood before her wanting to say something, but couldn't. In that instant, after days of anxiety, I was very happy, for we had guests but my mother and I were alone together. It was like the festival of the New Year. My father's eyes in the photo on the mantle had a sad look. Perhaps that was the first day I looked very closely at my father's picture. I imagined that he was looking at me and I wished my mother would say something about him, but she was silent. She was wearing a knitwear dress as red as jujube, her curly blonde hair hanging over her shoulders. Her lips were pursed like the times when she was not on speaking terms with me, and a small dimple had formed in her chin.

She cast a passing glance at me. Instantly, all my faith in her returned. Once again I was light-hearted and began jumping up and down in the air. When she was done, I followed her to the reception room, but as we reached the basement, I let go of her and decided to go see Granma. I went downstairs and saw Granma standing by the stove, her face shining with small beads of sweat. She wiped her eyes with the corner of her kerchief and said, "Don't come in here, sweetie. It's all smoky, it'll burn your eyes." Then, she bent over to pick up a couple small meatballs which she had fried for *Fesenjan* from the plate and gave them to me. She looked at me for a moment as I ate the meatballs, she hugged me and held my head to her bosom. I inhaled the familiar endearing smell of her body; her kerchief smelled of smoke.

I could not look at her face. In a trembling voice, I asked, "Granma, tonight, my father's coming tonight?" I kept my head pressed to her chest. I could feel her heart beating next to my cheek. I was all anticipation and regretted asking this question. How I wished she would take her time to answer. The longing to hear her say, "Yes, he's coming" choked my heart and visions of the future were racing through my head. But Granma wasn't saying anything. I was afraid to raise my head and look at her face, but she seemed to be trembling and I could hear her breathing faster. She pressed me to her chest and warm tears dropped on my forehead. Time seemed to be moving so slowly. As if night had fallen and the guests had all gone home. She lifted my head and held my face in her hands. She looked at me for a moment and wiped my eyes with her rough thumbs. Her wrinkles seemed deeper, though the resemblance to my mother was still visible in spite of them.

Softly she said, "It's too smoky in here. Go upstairs, go on my child. Go get some sweets from your uncle." She bent over. I pressed my face to her cheek, which was moist and quivering. Behind her kerchiefed head, the reflection of the flames and shadows on the soot-covered walls reminded me of Hell. I asked her, "Granma, are you crying?" A bitter sigh broke in her chest. She shook and did not answer. I thought that despite all those vows I had made to myself, I was still a meddlesome girl. I left Granma and climbed upstairs without uttering a word. Half way up the stairs, I turned around to look at her. She was turning the skimmer in the pot and her face glistened like the stars. As she placed another piece of firewood under the pot, her face suddenly turned crystalline red and then disappeared in the smoke and darkness.

I ran towards the reception room, which was packed with family members. Then a man with a long beard came in, wearing a thin black *aba* over his shoulders and a muslin turban on his head. Along with him came a goateed dwarf carrying a big register under his arm, a book that was large out of all proportion to his height. Both of them went towards the corner room where my mother was sitting in front of the full-size mirror, her face shining with the light of the lamps. She stole a glance at me and I rose to jump into her arms, but she bit her lip, pinning me to my seat.

There were doubts in her glance and I was dumbfounded by her beauty. I was already missing her. After so many days of not being close to her, I wanted to talk to her; I had so much to tell her. The smoke of the wild rue,[3] the frightening voice of the bearded man and the hush which had suddenly fallen over the room held me back. At this point my mother looked at me again, but it was different from her usual look. This was how she would look at me to make up after a fight or to forgive me after catching me with my

---

[3] Wild rue is burned as a ritual measure for avoiding or counteracting the effects of the evil eye. It was traditionally burned on a happy occasion such as a marriage or birth to prevent an envious on-looker from causing a jinx.

finger in the jam jar. But she had not done anything wrong. I wanted to hug and kiss her and tell her all that was in my heart, about all the promises and vows, but my mother looked down again, at the Koran, and whispered something under her breath. The sound of clapping and the women's trilling cries of congratulation arose; I was frightened by the noise and I don't know who embraced me from behind and handed me a big *Berenji* cookie.

*****

About two weeks after my mother got married, I began to realize that there was someone else in the house besides us. My mother was treating me better; she herself would give me jam and some loose change. She would tell me stories at night and sleep beside me. I was in the habit of laying my head in the hollow of her arm and sleeping with my arm on her breast. I was so used to the smell of her body that I could fall sleep only in her arms. Perhaps I was a scaredy cat, but my mother had never left me alone at night and things were not much different when I was with Granma. But with my mother, it was special. With her next to me, I was not afraid of anything. That night I dreamed that a black hairy hand was reaching for me. I was all curled up and the hand was dragging me towards a ditch, which was like a furnace. Later, I realized that it was like the furnace of the *Taftuni* bakery in our neighborhood. The neighbor kids and I used to drop pebbles into it.

In the middle of the dream, I suddenly thought of the fate of bad people on the Day of Resurrection. The hairy hand was holding a fiery pick-axe, wanting to smash my head in with it. I tried to shout but couldn't. I was being relentlessly dragged towards the mouth of the furnace. My hands and feet were rubbery and numb; I could not control them. All of a sudden, I saw my mother who seemed to be standing on the other side of the furnace. She had the same knitted jujube dress on. She turned to me and bit her lip. I stretched my hand towards her. I was so happy to see her that I had forgotten that I was scared. I grabbed her skirt, which stretched in my hand, while she herself glided away from me. With a muffled cry I awoke. For a moment I did not know where I was. I could still feel the warmth of the flames on my cheeks. My body was shaking and my heart pounded as though it would fly right out my throat. Gradually I realized that it was only a nightmare, but I could not move. I remembered my mother and turned to embrace her. My fear had gone, when all at once I realized that my mother was no longer lying beside me.

For a while I could not lift the covers from my face; I dared not look at the darkness of the room. I felt that I was lying in somebody else's bed. Eventually I lifted my head out from under the covers. On the other side of the room, my mother and that man were sleeping. The satin-lined, floral-pattern quilt covering them was a keepsake of my mother's first marriage that I liked very much. My mother had laid her head upon that man's arm and her disheveled blonde hair fell over the pillow. Some of her curls looked blue in the moonlight.

*****

In the summer they sent me back to Granma's house. Although I had not done anything wrong, I knew that I was losing my mother to that man. She was very kind to me, like before, but I had a feeling that I no longer had the right to be with her like I used to. Her face was changing, her body was getting round and heavy. She lumbered about and no longer sang, and when she told me stories, there was an impatience in her voice. She would cut the stories short, omitting the details in the middle. I would not look at her either; I would pretend that I was asleep. She would get up with difficulty and sigh. She seemed to be exhausted and I was very happy when they sent me to Granma's house.

At Granma's house I could go back to playing the same games with my old playmates. The best thing about it was that I could be like I used to be, pretending that nothing at all had happened. My only problem was my uncle's spoiled and naughty child. In order to avoid him, I would play all by myself. I made myself a little vegetable patch, digging a water channel for it, drawing borders around it with the end of the broomstick, and planting vegetables. Mostly I loved to watch the garden. Once again the wild tulips and chamomiles had blossomed; the berry tree near the Snake Stable had spread its umbrella of leaves. Under the jujube tree, in place of the old russet goat was a curly black lamb, constantly bleating. The afternoons were the only bad part about those long days, because I could not sleep. I wanted to bathe in the bathing-pond, but Granma would not let me. She would tease me, as she called it, tell me a story, anything to make me fall sleep, but gradually she would tire and doze off. The buzzing of the flies and the white shadow of the bleached azure curtains would drive me crazy. Looking at the languid handsome face in the huge por-trait on the wall, my patience would run out. In front of the closet hung a canvas curtain on which was printed a picture depicting *Shirin* bathing herself as Khosrow, on horseback, bites his finger in admiration of her. Beyond them in the background were bluish mountain peaks, on top of which stood Farhad, facing them, his pick in hand. There were a few lines of poems written on the lower part of the curtain. I would make faces at them, tying the corner of Granma's kerchief to cast a spell on the daughter of the fairy king, causing her to wander far from home. I kept all this from Granma. I would play with the bag of money hanging from her neck; I liked the jingling sound of the money. But, after a while, I would get thoroughly bored. I would make faces at Granma, who was asleep, and imitate her snoring. I would toss and turn until she woke up. She would place her heavy hand around my neck to make me "drop dead," as she would say.

*****

One day I was tossing and turning like that as I lay beside Granma. Someone knocked on the door; my uncle had returned. Granma was sound asleep. Even if she woke up, I would tell her that I was going to go to my uncle's room. I took her hand off my neck and got up. I stood on the veranda of my uncle's room. He took a big apricot out of the brown bag he was holding in his hand and gave it to me. Then, he caressed me on the head. At this mo-ment, his naughty boy ran towards us, pushed me back and em-braced his father by hanging from his neck. My uncle hugged him, held him up in his hands and looked at him for a while. The kid's face was dirty and his gaze was fixed and meaningless. My uncle kissed him a few times and gave him a ride on his shoulders around the room, and said a few times, "How much I missed you, my child! Since this morning... When I left, you were asleep. How much I missed you..." His voice gradually faded away. The taste of the sour apricot turned to a burning sensation in my mouth; I ran towards the courtyard and spit it out in the foot-bath, and I do not know how it happened that I went into the garden.

As usual, there was nobody in the garden at that time of the day. I do not know why I went under the berry tree; I sat on the smashed leaves and stirred them up with a dry blade of grass. The beetles and crickets had threaded a circle around me with their sharp constant noise. The strong smell of the smashed decaying leaves mixed with the aroma of common dill, chamomile and parsley and made the hot afternoon air heavier. It was as if I was falling sleep; my limbs were weakened and the scenery around me seemed to be fading away. Under the sunlight, the saplings and flowers trembled as they grew to meet the sun. All of a sudden, everything I had seen before a hundred times seemed new to me. The dome and the minaret seemed to fade away; the cob-plastered facade of the rooftop of our house seemed to be getting miles away from me. I was not interested in anything. I felt that I was going down a narrow pass. My body had become one-ply and thin-skinned like the Dasteh Aloo dolls. I longed for some cool air but I could not find any; it was as if a weight had been placed on my chest.

I lifted my head from my knees and stopped drawing lines on the smashed leaves. Then, suddenly I noticed that the Snake Stable was right in front of me and it was a hot afternoon... I had never been so close to it; I gazed at its glassless windows.

Something was there, behind the empty window pane: two oblique eyes of the snake, red and shining. Its gaze was fixed and bright. Every now and then, a green flash sparkled in its glassy spiralling eyes. We stared at each other for a while. I was neither scared by it, nor was it foreign to me. I closed my eyes for a moment and drowned myself in my inner darkness. There was nothing...nothing.

When I opened my eyes, the snake was still looking at me. It gazed at me with a look full of lonely grief.

The darkness was coming on.

Shahrnush Pârsipur was born in 1946 to a Tehrani housewife and a lawyer from Shiraz. She grew up with three younger brothers, which she feels accounts for her having been something of a tomboy. She went to grade school in Tehran and spent her high school years in Khorramshahr, where she began working at age 18 as a typist and telephone operator for the Water and Power Company. Eventually she returned to Tehran, where she obtained a B.A. in social sciences from the University of Tehran. Parsipur married, had a son and subsequently divorced in 1973. She worked for a while in Iranian television but was arrested in 1974, and two years later, due to the increasing political troubles within Iran, left the country. She stayed in France for two years, where she studied Chinese language and philosophy.

She remembers being an avid reader, along with her mother, from early childhood. She began writing her own stories from about the age of 13, and had published a few items under a pseudonym in various journals while still in her teens. Since then, she has published three novels, four collections of short stories, a story book for children and a number of articles, including a book of literary criticism. Her first novel, *The Dog and the Long Winter* (*Sag va zemestân-e boland*), which she began at about the age of 20, was completed in the summer of 1974 and published to critical acclaim. *Women Without Men* (*Zanân bedun-e mardân*), a novella consisting of inter-related short stories about different women who all find their way to a house outside Tehran where only women reside, though written just after her divorce in the mid 1970s, was not published until 1989. The Islamic Republic of Iran banned this book and pressured Parsipur to change her focus from overtly feminist issues. Parsipur had already spent four years in prison during the mid-1980s, during which time she wrote her second novel, *Tuba and the Meaning of Night* (*Tubâ va ma'nâ-ye shab*), also published in 1989 to considerable critical acclaim. *The Blue Intellect* (`*Aql-i âbî*), Parsipur's most recent novel, was written in 1989, but could not be published in Iran. It was published in the United States, as was her most recent collection of short stories, *Tea Ceremony in the Pres-*

ence of the Wolf (*Adâb-i sarf-e chây dar hozur-e gorg*). Parsipur won the Hellman-Hammett Prize in 1994 and is currently on an extended visit to the United States, where she is living in Los Angeles.

The Heat of the Year Zero ("*Garmâ dar sâl-e sefr*") in *Avizehha-ye bolur* (Tehran: Inteshârât-e Râz, 1977, pp. 45-49) was published as the unrest which led to the revolution of 1979 was picking up. It illustrates a young girl's experience of the heat and boredom of summer in pre-revolutionary Iran and her response to the circumstances which shape and determine her life, and eventually constrain her close relationship with her brother.

"*The Men of Aramaea*" ("*Mardân-e Ârâm*" in *Âdâb-e sarf-e chây dar hozur-e gorg* [(Los Angeles and San Jose: Tasveer and Nashr-e Zamâneh, 1993], pp. 161-4), written in Iowa City in September of 1992, treats the theme of love, loss and exile in a magical realist vein. It is one of a series of interconnected stories named for ancient civilizations that appear in her collection *Tea Ceremony in the Presence of the Wolf*. At the same time that the Persian word *ârâm* is associated with the Aramaic civilization, it is also the common word for calm or tranquility, so that the title can also be understood as "the men of tranquility" or "the calm men." The story alludes to a real incident, reported widely in the press, of an Iranian girl who died when her fiance tried to smuggle her into the U.S. in his suitcase.

3

The Heat of the Year Zero

Shahrnush Parsipur

The summer when I was sixteen, mother finally got tired of it. We were working all morning, arranging and tidying the furniture and sprinkling naphthalene over all the rooms to keep away the moths. As mother was opening the drawing room drapes, she sat down on the stool she was standing on to reach them and said, "O let's not go, after all. I don't feel like it." I thought she was going to cry now, but I heard only the sound of her breathing in the silence.

So we didn't go, but remained in the heat. From then on, we'd gather together in the afternoons in a room that had an air conditioner. I tried at such times to put up with the heat, and would go to my room and stretch out naked on my bed. The smell of musty naphthalene wafts from the drawing room as I just lay there counting the beads of sweat dripping onto my pillow from the strands of my hair or looking out the window at the heat as it melts on the wall tops and sticks to the ground. Like a rotting corpse. At sunset, I would go up on the roof and walk on the humid cob while breathing in the steamy air and just count the lone stars twinkling in the pure, open, sadly-tinged background of the sky. And the sky was cobalt blue.

On sweltering nights I heard the voice of the gypsy woman singing in the casino a couple hundred meters down below. On those sweltering nights the air feels like a wave. You have to strain to hear sounds. That's how it was and we put up with it. I kept to myself, crouched up in a ball like a new-born chick.

My mother would say, "You look just like an owl. When I was your age, I spun around like a top on a brick," and she'd puff on her cigarette. She was tired herself. I could tell. Then she'd go in her room sometimes and lock the door behind her and crouch on the bed. We could see her through the window. We children would go and stand at the window, analyzing her moods. I'd stand by the door and look at the men from the docks waiting in front of the consulate to talk with Saleh Ghorbavi.

Spangles of sweat shone on their skin and their undershirts were soiled, completely filthy. When they passed close by, they smelled of mold and sunshine and the ship's hold. I'd count them, one two, three...eight and so on, all through the night. Or I'd track the lights of the cars and keep watch of how many passed by. There weren't many cars, nor were there many people. The heat scared them off. Sometimes in the afternoons we'd go to the river and walk along its banks. The heels of our shoes would sink into the asphalt and I felt as if the humidity meant to split right through our skin and meat and form dew on our bones. I liked to read books, so I did. Then I'd think of the north and the sea. My thoughts would flutter to the mountains around Tehran and Karaj and the river which poured forcefully over the rocks. Here the river rolls calmly by and awakened no feelings of youth or vigor in me. I never longed to swim in its lapping water. Maybe it's because those damn sharks are lying in wait everywhere.

Finally, after all this, when there was nothing left to think of, I'd get onto the subject of men. I was tired and it seemed to me I'd grown old. I felt I was beginning to decompose. I'd go before the mirror and take my clothes off. I looked at my figure in the mirror, drenched in sweat and yellowing. I looked like the pimples on my forehead. In the lamplight, I felt sorry for myself, so I'd turn out the lamp and there would be only the heat, and no light.

That's why I'd stand by the door and think about the men from the docks, about all the men of the world. As they approached from a distance, I'd tell myself, "I'll jump in his arms and tell him to take me with him, wherever he takes me. We'll go to the moun-

tains and get a hut with a swimming pool in front, or a spring—
and two or three cold-weather trees. Whatever it is, we'll lay en-
twined together and be mates."

That's how my thoughts went, but they never came true. The
men would pass by and I would look at them, but they had no
yen for me, nor I for them. Something was dying or had died, or
all of us together—the men, the river and the earth—were decom-
posing. Once a drunken Indian called out imploringly to me as he
passed, "Hey, baby," and tottered in my direction. I fled inside the
house. And so on and so forth, and I still heard the sound of that
gypsy at nights. They used to say that blood had been spilled in
the name of that gypsy and that all the chauffeurs were fighting
over her.

We were stuck at a crossroads, the crossroads of my mother
and the heat. My mother would say, "It's better like this. A body's
whole life is here. Of course, there's the heat, but you've got your
whole life at your fingertips; your carpets are there, your table and
chairs here, the walls of your own house all around you. And,
after all, the heat doesn't last till the end of time, does it?" I knew
full well that it would last until the end of the summer, not till the
end of time, but there were three full months until the end of
summer...We'd tell fortunes with cards and I'd lay designs on men
whom I had seen once in my life.

Then, when they caught my brother in the storeroom, the whole
situation changed. They'd taken him to the police station. They
said he'd tried to steal goods from a barge. Father went and pulled
some strings to bring him home. Then he pulled out his belt to
whip him. My brother took off like a shooting star and flew up
onto the roof, into the strong room and finally, into the streets,
where he stayed until past midnight. It was there that the fuss
over the event died down.

After that, we leagued together. My brother and I would swipe
two or three cartons of beer and take it up on the roof. It was
sweltering and in the steamy air we breathed and drank beer. The
beer was lukewarm and bitter, and it turned our stomachs, but we
chugged away at it and got smashed. We'd talk about the stars
and look around in the blue of the sky for things that didn't even
exist. We agreed to go in tandem and sign up as deck hands on

one of the ships. Then my brother shook his head in sorrow, saying, "But you, you can't come, can you?" "No," I'd say. He'd shake his head again. "We could have gotten on swell together."

Sometimes we'd go out on the jetty and sit across from our house, watching the Arabs on their barges in the light of their cooking fires and look at the white birds on the water and listen to the ships' horns. My brother would tell me stories about the nights when he went over to eat dinner with them. He swore he had not gone to steal anything that night, only out of curiosity. And I thought that I'd go, too, if the heat and loneliness didn't hold me back. Then we'd gaze in silence for a while at the tide flowing out and when it flowed back in, the stars would come out one by one and sometimes the moon, which, because of the heat, looked like a knot in the bark of a poplar tree, stuck to the roof of the sky. My brother was saying that these barges go all the way to India. He said that one of his buddies was on the water for nine months and then jumped ship when he got to Bandar Abbas. One or two days later he became distraught over it. My brother waved his hands animatedly in the muggy air: "Think of it, he runs all the way here from Bandar Abbas in an instant!" I asked, "So why did he run? Couldn't he rent a car or something?"

"I don't know." As he was saying this, he looked downward in anger. His heart was itching for the sea and he wanted to believe that his buddy had run here all the way from Bandar Abbas. I sensed this myself. I could sense a lot of things, but I listened quietly. He was someone to talk to, anyhow. Losing hold of him was a kind of tragedy in that heat and that silence, I felt like a pane of glass held in place by the window frame. I could feel it and I kept it to myself so he wouldn't know. I was nonchalant. In order not to lose hold on him, I was nonchalant and I tried not to express an opinion that would upset him and drive him away from me. Later on he went out less with me and more with his buddies.

Later on I found out that they would go to the riverside to pick up girls. That's why I couldn't go along the jetty anymore and watch the Arabs and experience the birds and the barges up close. I just stood by the sea and kept an eye on the longshoremen and counted the passing car lights. At sunset I'd go on the roof and breathe in the steamy air, count the lone stars and listen to the voice of that gypsy at night singing in the casino down there, with people spilling blood over her....and I read.

The next summer my mother said, "We'll go, I'm fed up." she was closing her suitcase and said this to bolster her resolve. She sat on the suitcase. We looked at her and I thought, "She'll cry now," but I only heard the sound of her breathing. Then she added, "It's true that a person is in his own house with his life at his fingertips, his carpets are over there and his rooms are all around him. But then there's the heat, of course. You know?"

We knew it, and that's why we left.

4

The Men of Aramaea

Sharnoush Parsipur

In the civilization of Aramaea, a wondrous calm would have reigned, except for the girl who fell in love. Girls have no right to fall in love, for in doing so they cause much havoc. This girl was in love with a man who played the *târ*, and this man who played the *târ* was a captive of two men, one who had a beard and another who had shaved his beard.

The girl tried very hard to free her beloved. At first she thought to turn herself to smoke and enter through the crack between the door and the doorjamb, encircle her beloved, turn him to smoke and escape together through the crack at the door. She next thought to shrink herself to the size of a single atom or molecule and then go in and steal him away. Third, she thought to go and beg for his release. None of these proved possible, for although the civilization of Eram was formerly quite splendid, it was not possible even in that culture to turn to smoke or into an atom. Begging for his release was no good either, because her beloved did not like begging and it might make him hate her. And so the girl paced day and night, thinking.

Then one day a man told her that her beloved had escaped and was now in Turkey, anxiously awaiting to see her. The girl went nearly mad with joy and hardly noticed how she made her way to Turkey. A man there told her that her beloved had been compelled to set out in secret under the cover of night with a forged passport for Germany. He had left instructions for the girl to remain in Turkey until such time as she could find a way to enter Germany. She obeyed and got a job as a sales clerk in a clothing shop and then, to make sure that no one could touch her, she changed her job eight times and lost all trace of her beloved and all trace of herself as well. But because love, like musk, cannot be hidden, one day she met a man in the street who knew her fiance. "Where have you been, Miss?," the man asked her. "Your beloved has three times arranged for you to go to Germany, but we couldn't find you."

The girl, in lieu of an answer, just cried. The man, who felt sorry for her, said that he could get her to Germany now, but the problem was that her lover had gone to Canada and was waiting there for a visa to America. The girl, who was patient, went to Germany and washed dishes in a restaurant. Two years passed by, during which the two of them exchanged correspondence and even talked on the phone a few times. The man said that when he got to America he would make *târs* and sell them and they would become millionaires. As a result, the girl agreed to knit sweaters in the evenings after dishwashing and sell them to the women in the neighborhood.

But her lover shivered for a good long while in the cold of Canada and worked as an attendant in parking garages at night and never found time to make *târs* and become rich. So, he entered America illegally and went to California, where, unexpectedly, a situation occured that made it possible for him to become a legal resident, because he had been received as an artist, for he was now making *târs* and selling them. He phoned the girl and told her, "I am coming," and he came.

The two of them were in a hotel and no place outside of that hotel existed. Because they were in the only place that was and no one else existed except for them, every once in a while the sound of music could be heard in the distance and every once in a while some people would pass by beneath their window talking to one another. But did any place on earth exist? America? Well, what difference did it make? They were there, the two of them, the room was there. What else could they want?

The man said, "I will put you in the suitcase and take you." He bought a suitcase and put the girl in it. The girl was cold in the suitcase, flying through the air. Before falling deep asleep, she returned to the room in the hotel and fell into the man's embrace.

In the airport in America, the people found a suitcase with a girl inside who had fallen deep asleep.

The *târ*-playing man from the civilization of Eram spoke about missles for some time and then invented a *târ* that was like a violin. He took it with him to Lake Tahoe, for he wanted to play violin for the people gambling there. But because the girl had plunged within him, he had now become a woman playing the violin. Give this, he invented a strap to go around his head that would hold a wind instrument to his mouth. He played the violin and a wind instrument together and, at the same time, he sang in a feminine register. He even sang in the language of the Americans, though no one listened to him. The people gambled and the slot-machines whirred.

The girl, who was within the man, wanted to wear a dress of turquoise, and she did. The dress was beautiful and the girl continued to play the violin and blow into the wind instrument. The man said, "How beautiful you are! Let's go out on the lake in a boat."

They went. The girl sang. The man was all ears. Afterwards he got up and embraced the girl and they rolled together in the water. The lake was so blue it was unreal.

Moniru Ravânipur was born in 1954 in the village of Jofreh and was raised in the city of Shiraz and graduated from Shiraz University with a B.A. in psychology. Ravânipur's first novel, *The People of Gharq* (*Ahl-e gharq*), published in 1989, established her as one of Iran's best contemporary writers. This novel, like most of Ravânipur's writing, takes as its subject the rituals, customs and traditions of the villagers of the coastal region of the Persian Gulf and the small towns in southern Iran. A collection of her short stories, *Kanizu*, was also published in the same year. In 1990 a second novel, *Heart of Steel* (*Del-e fulâd*), appeared, followed by a second collection of short stories, *The Stones of Satan* (*Sang-hâ-ye Shaytân*). A third collection of short stories, *Siriyâ, Siriyâ*, was written after her trip to the Northern island of Ashuradeh and the Southern islands of Qeshm and Hengâm. Ravânipur currently lives in Iran.

In the story, *"Acting"* (*"Bâzi"*) in the collection *Sang-hâ-ye Shaytân* (Tehran: Nashr-e Markaz, 1991, pp. 63-67), Ravânipur draws the portrait of an aspiring actress who allows an opportunistic director to take sexual advantage of her, but is unsuccessful in engaging his professional attention or admiration.

In the second story by Ravânipur, *"We Only Fear the Future"* (*"Mâ faqat az âyandeh mi-tarsim"*) in the same collection, pp. 35-42, she humorously illustrates the effects of segregation and infatuation of a group of adolescent boys when they discover a mysterious female painter in the building across from their hangout.

Ravânipur's third story *"Mânâ, Kind Mânâ"* (*"Mânâ, Mânâ-ye mehrebân"*) in *Kanizu* (Tehran: Enteshârât-e Nilufar, 1989, pp. 97-104) deals once again with the relations between the sexes, this time in a magical-realistic mode, with the Iran-Iraq War as the background.

5

Acting
Moniru Ravanipur

The bothersome, stubborn, persistent wind whirled around the bare branch of the tree in an effort to detach the last leaf. It was the last month of autumn. Maryam was watching from behind the fence; the girl was still sitting on the steps in front of the building of the College of Literature. The autumn wind was hoisting the fallen leaves up into the air.

Maryam got up lethargically and grabbed her briefcase, which was full of books and papers. She went towards the tree and stood under it, raised her hand to reach the dried leaf, and detached it. She heard the rustle of the leaf being crushed in her fist and smiled. She began walking along the fence surrounding the College of Literature. She heard the low-pitched sound of the bell and felt anxious. She entered the courtyard of the building. The girl, hesitant and helpless, was getting up; her eyes were red and puffy. Maryam climbed up the stairs. The posters of previously-shown plays were still on the walls. While glancing at the posters, Maryam saw the man, who was coming from the opposite end of the hallway, briefcase in hand. He had a blue checkered shirt on. His long, loose hair had fallen on his shoulders. The man was approaching Maryam, paying no attention to the girl who had reached him. The girl was waving her hands and wiping her cheeks. She was being dragged behind the man.

Maryam turned towards an old poster on the wall, it was three months old... She read the names: The Director... The Actors... The Actress... She restlessly put her hand inside her briefcase, grabbed a book and took it out. She shook her head, zipped up her briefcase and returned to the hallway.

The hallway was crowded. The man was trying to find his way through the crowd. The girl was following him very closely. She had put her hand over her mouth; her shoulders were trembling.

The man, who had reached Maryam, smiled, took a long breath and said, "Did I keep you waiting?"

As they were leaving the building of the College of Literature, Maryam saw the girl leaning against the wall, hiding her face in both hands. As usual, the man turned right and headed towards *Hafezieh.* He had frowned; he seemed to be tired.

"She can't act... I've told her a hundred times..."

"Was she in the last play?" Maryam asked.

"Yes, but beauty isn't the only thing. I need a good voice for this role. A strong voice..."

Maryam pulled herself up to her full height, wiped the smile off her face, opened her briefcase and took the script out. "I've memorized all of the dialogues."

"Leave it for later... after we've rested."

They had reached the gate of Hafezieh. The man stroked his blonde beard and stopped at the fence surrounding the garden. The wind was scattering the last rose petals.

"What terrible weather! There's too much dust in the air..." The man was exhausted. He could hardly talk; he was stuttering. He was not looking at Maryam as he usually did. "My place is very close by. I've made hot tea. You can rehearse a couple of scenes there..."

*****

Maryam said, "Let's talk about the play."

The man rolled over and answered wearily, "Now? Let's do it later."

No sound could be heard from the alley. The wind was driving the rain drops against the window panes. Maryam looked at the man's blonde hair, the drops of sweat on his forehead and his white-skinned body lying beside her. The man's eyes were closed. Maryam touched his forehead and asked him, "Do you think I can?"

In the same position, his eyes still closed, the man asked, "What is it that you can?"

"Can I play Antigone?!"[4]

The man, sleepy, whispered, "Yeah, yeah... you can..." and began snoring. Expecting an answer, Maryam looked at him. The man's snoring had became more regular.

Maryam softly asked, "Are you asleep?"

She spread a sheet over the man's naked body to cover it — the body which she was now embarrassed to see.

She turned her face away. The room was small and painted in gray. A few books were scattered on the floor here and there. The picture of an old man with spectacles and a goatee was hanging on the wall. Maryam kept a distance from the man, grabbed a book and opened it:

"I love you as much as I love all the women whom I have never met. Your belly..." [5]

She impatiently closed the book, lay on her stomach and put her arm under her chin. Through the window the sky looked dark. It was drizzling. Heavy-hearted, she looked at the man. With two of her long, slender fingers she pulled up the man's eyelid and saw the blue unaffectionate pupil of his eye. The man did not move. Maryam withdrew her hand. Once again, she looked at the picture of the old man wearing glasses and the books scattered around. She impatiently sat up and loudly said, "Well, now..." Then, she cheerfully gazed at the wall. An ant was climbing up the wall. She blocked its way:

"How are you doing? Where are you going? Let's talk. No, don't go. I don't want to hurt you. I just want to talk to you. Have

---

[4] The famous tragedy by *Sophocles*.

[5] From a book of poems by Octavio Paz entitled, "*Piedra de sol*" (1957; translated to English as *Sun Stone*, 1963).

you ever been to the theater? Have you? You may have wandered around between the aisles. If you haven't been to the theater, you should know that I... am an actress and this guy, who's asleep, is a director... Where are you going? Do you want me to show you the script?... Would you like me to read it for you? Listen: 'In my sorrow, no one's sigh would rise up to the heaven, no one's tear drops would fall down on the earth...' Stop! I swear to God that I won't hurt you. Yes, now... We've become friends today... You know, we shouldn't take things too seriously... He says that I can act... He himself said that... What do you think? Don't go... What kind of friend are you? Is his snoring frightening you? Are you afraid of... Stop... Stop! I want to show you the script..."

*****

The ant was running away... The rain was pouring down and the man was snoring.

6

We Only Fear the Future

Moniru Ravanipur

We were poets with nothing to reminisce about. Every afternoon, from, oh let's say about 4 p.m., we would stand on that street in front of the bookstore talking. We'd read poetry and debate. That's how it was every day. The words were not real, they just seemed to hover around us like a swarm of flies and when we'd reach the bookseller's, they'd circle around our heads all abuzz. And then, if we got tired, there was a café next to the bookseller where we'd sit drinking tea, and then the buzzing sound would circle through the café until our jaw muscles would tire, at which point we'd get up and leave.

Across from the bookseller, on the other side of the street, was a row of shops with apartments above. We'd never realized they were there, but on that day, we finally saw them.

Maybe it was a Saturday. The reason I say maybe is because we were all confused by what happened and to this day we don't really know what day it was or wasn't. But we all are sure of this, that she was not there before. Not in that apartment above the shop across the way with its little door opening onto the street—a door which we were seeing for the first time—nor anywhere in town. In a small town like that, if there were a woman, and especially one like her, we would certainly have known it. We were poets and were after experience, and a woman who wore black from head to toe and did not tie her kerchief, so that sometimes—but not always—the white of her neck could be seen, was beyond the experience of any of us. We could tell from the excited glances we exchanged with one another; our eyes sparkled that day, all of those days...

It was four o'clock the first time she came out of her house. She had an oval face, thin, pursed lips and black hair, which must have been quite long, reaching to her waist if it were let loose. There was a cloud of grief over her face, or, perhaps because she was wearing black we imagined she was sad, and it made us sad, too.

When she crossed to our side of the street, following the cars with a pleasing motion of her head and neck, and entered the bookstore, we suddenly remembered we should check to see if there were any new books, though we hadn't been reading books for some while and had not been visiting the bookstore. It was there that we began supposing that she wanted the works of Van Gogh. Her voice made us dizzy and we were no longer listening to what she said—maybe we didn't listen from the first. They were just words, brilliant, translucent words, gliding through the air, and we reached the conclusion that she was a painter wanting to buy an easel and paints and canvas.

When she left, the bookstore seemed empty. There was nothing left for us to do. We came out, but it was if we didn't know one another anymore and had no idea why we used to stand around there together or what we used to talk about.

It was that same day, I think, that we saw the small door open once again. A moment later we could see the drapes, which were faded, and we supposed that the room must be quite large because large rooms always have big sliding glass doors, and that it must be the studio where she paints, a place facing the street which, when the sun climbed the sky, would be full of light. Naturally, you need light in order to paint.

When we came back the next day we saw that the drapes were new. Decorated all over with sea birds, birds that had flown far inland and lost their way and no longer knew which direction to return. The movement of the neck and head of these sea birds seemed to ask us for directions to the sea. That's why we started talking about sea birds and then crowded into the bookstore to see what books there are about the ocean and sea birds. We wanted to find out how sea birds find their way around, just to know and not to worry.

It took a whole week before we stopped talking about the ocean and sea birds and occupied ourselves with other things. Maybe we would have talked about sea birds like that even if the drapes had not been a little short and we couldn't see her shins, which made it clear she was sitting facing the street. But on the eighth day, we saw she was sitting, once again evidently facing the street, because we could see the hem of her black skirt, which reached to her mid-calf and a hand which, every now and then picked something from the floor. We knew her brush must have fallen or a tube of paint or one of her sketching pencils...

When it got dark that day, we all left and felt shooting pains in our shins until morning. The next day we came earlier than usual and saw that she was not there. She wasn't there and it wasn't until a quarter to three that we saw her legs. She came and sat on the chair. She adjusted the position of the chair a bit and started working. Two or three times her brush or her pencil fell...we saw her hand, so white and sweet.

For ten days we stood there like that, watching. No one knew what she was drawing. But we always watched to see if the curtains would rustle and they did. And so we'd come every day at a quarter to three, stand outside the bookstore or sometimes we'd come a bit earlier to the café to drink some tea. The tea tasted better there; none of us was drinking tea at home anymore. Precisely at sixteen minutes to three we'd leave the café and take up our posts.

That day she drew aside the drapes. The eleventh day. We saw she had taken her painting off the easel. She put another canvas on it and, without closing the drapes, sat on the chair. We looked at each other, unbelieving, our eyes all aglow as though we had been released from some great torment. Our breath quickened and we cast furtive glances in her direction while pretending to be occupied with something else. We saw her, sometimes backing away from the canvas and then getting closer... and we knew that she was looking out and we were certain that she was painting the face and figure of one of us.

For this reason, we repeated the pose and gestures of the previous days, because we supposed that if she had painted up to a certain point yesterday, for example, if one of us had waved our hand in the air, then we had best repeat the movement so she could complete the painting.

Because we knew nothing about painting and how long it takes before a sketch is completed or a picture takes shape on the canvas, we went to the bookstore and bought and read all the books on painting and the techniques of painting and the biographies of the great painters and grew pretty comfortable except for one thing: that our hair was getting longer and our beards were growing, which of course, we could not control, but we tried to control everything as much as possible, and this problem would occur to us every now and then because we were constantly looking at one another's hair and beard. We were apprehensive and full of dread that she might close the drapes and leave forever.

And one day two months later, after we had tired of standing on one corner repeating our poses and gestures, she seemed to sense it and suddenly got up, removed the canvas from the easel and put another one in its place. This time we stood on the other side of the shop and tried to do something so she could draw us in a different scene, and helped her to complete her work quickly and without blemish by repeating our gestures and actions.

We filled up our days like this, and at night, when the bookstore closed, she would get up and close the drapes, and we would walk off together. We couldn't take leave of each other, as if we didn't want to be lonely or were afraid that something might suddenly happen, or that it already had and one of us might not know about it. That's why we took turns, and I couldn't say how we arranged it as none of us had said a word, sitting around in each other's houses draining the bottle. First we just sipped it, as no one wanted to drink more than any of the others. We wanted to have our wits about us in case someone decided to say something, so that the words would not go unheard...but no one had much to say, only about paints and canvas and painting and Cezanne and Van Gogh and... We would talk about what we had just learned, dwelling on Van Gogh's amputated ear, which we were sure was a white, sweet lobe, and because of this very fact, we'd sometimes cry.

Late at night each one of us would sprawl out in a corner and for a while we'd hear our loud lengthy sighs and we knew that each of us, in the drunken state of half-wakefulness, was reviewing our gestures and poses of earlier in the day so that tomorrow we could recapture them and not disturb her work.

After a while we realized that she sometimes came to the bookstore between 2 p.m. and a quarter to three. So we would mostly come around one o'clock...she'd come, give her head a little shake, look at the books. She didn't buy anything and we thought she was looking at us, giving us the once over to see if we all had come or not...So, without talking about it amongst ourselves, from then on we all showed up there at one o'clock, and after one week of coming at one o'clock, we saw her smile. She seemed content. We smiled, too, amongst ourselves, stood there looking, stood in such a way that she could see all of us and look most at whichever one of us she most preferred.

Several times we saw her getting out of a taxi. A taxi or one of those delivery pickup trucks. Now we can't remember for sure, because she was carrying a parcel with her, a tripod or a board or something else. When she got out of the delivery truck, she had great difficulty carrying her parcel. We were standing there watching and saw the driver help her and before we could get ourselves in motion and step over to her, she opened the little door and let the driver take her things upstairs. We stared at each other in disbelief, stood there frozen like statues and saw the driver, who was young and dark-complexioned with a bushy moustache, put the money in his pocket as he came out and closed the little door behind himself. Before we could go talk with him, he got into his pickup, stepped on the gas, and was gone. That day we realized that not one of us knew how to drive, and we never did find the dark-complexioned driver after that, though we looked for him about town.

One time we straggled over to a point across from the door she had opened. Short steps, gray or dull metallic, and dark. We thought to ourselves that the light bulb in the stairwell must have burnt out, but none of us knew anything about electricity. That day we looked at the street lights and thought about the people who climbed the telephone polls and fixed the wires.

I clearly remember the day she left. A day on which we all suddenly aged and well....none of us saw her leaving, but she was gone. It must have been under the cover of darkness. She didn't go on Friday, because on Fridays[6] we would sometimes walk and once in a while take a taxi down her street, even though there was no one there and the curtains were drawn and there were no shins to be seen, but we would come anyway.

When she left our mutual neediness, our need to forget or to see her again drew us closer together. We talked together, talked about her, and talked openly. I don't know how, but we all understood that she had once loved someone or two people had fallen in love with her at the same time, and in the ensuing battle over her, they both get themselves killed, or maybe one of them kills the other and is sentenced to death for it in court. She, her house looking out onto Edam Square where the execution takes place, would always rise with the dawn and watch the sun climb the horizon. She saw the sleepy soldiers bringing the one who survived to prepare him for execution and he, walking before the soldiers, drew deep breaths...maybe hoping to catch her scent in the air. Or maybe the one who survived knew that she rose early every morning to experience the sunrise and stood wakeful many a night outside her window, waiting.

That's how we suddenly realized she had, from that moment on, clad in black and mourning, devoted herself to painting and thought to open galleries in different cities. That's why we always listened for news of the art world, and still listen, to see in which city the woman clad in black will exhibit her works.

For the first few months, we would go all together to the depot to ask if there was a woman dressed in black, a painter, among the passengers. But now we suppose that we have to go to the depot in turns, one at a time, to watch the passengers get off and report to the rest of us whether she has come or not....It's not too much trouble, no more trouble than what we experience when waking or

---

[6] Friday is the Sabbath day in Muslim countries, and work is generally suspended.

asleep. Though we don't let on, sometimes in our sleep we dream of falling asleep so as to stop thinking about her, but we are always awake in our dreams so that if we fall asleep, we are, in effect, awake and so it is difficult for us, more and more difficult every day. If she had gone up and closed the door and the curtains had covered the whole window, we wouldn't have come to this, because we know that even if we manage to get her out of our minds, one day she will return and hang those short drapes and we'll see her shins again and the hand reaching under the table to pick up the pencil or the brush which has fallen and then, once again, our shins start to ache.

With every passing day, even now as we speak, it fades further into the past, and no one can alter the past. That is, this moment, today, tomorrow and the days yet to come—these cannot be changed. And we know that fear, the fear that we bear within ourselves, is always there, it will not let us be, it has grown accustomed to us and is afraid to leave, almost as if, were it to leave, there is nowhere else for it to go, to live and breathe...That's why we are always afraid, afraid of the future, which is the past, afraid that she will come once more and think that we have forgotten her.

Tehran 28 Azar 1369 (18 December 1990)

7

Mânâ, Kind Mânâ
Moniru Ravanipur

ow could you not know?," I said. "The sea is full of sharks, sharks that look like ordinary fish, so much like fish, in fact, that you can't tell the difference until you're right up close to them, where you can smell their breath, and by then it's too late."

He laughed. He was sitting on this same black sofa in front of me, laughing. Then his glance happened to fall upon this flower-pot or maybe he just wanted to change the subject of conversation and he said, "Your marsh palm is shriveling up, you ought to water it."

"The marsh palm?," I said. "No...I don't like it."

He pushed the hair back off his forehead. "You people from Bushire are terrible!"

He would come whenever he was passing through Tehran. He would come to my house and we'd sit down to talk and read stories. He had come that day too and we swapped stories and now he had to go. It was getting dark and a star, a twinkling star, had risen to a point just outside the window and was hovering there in the sky.

I didn't know where his house was, or even what his name was. I was always fearful of knowing his name; when you've learned somebody's name, they have a way of falling away from you, you set them apart and we didn't want that, didn't want to be

apart and that's why I didn't know his name, nor he mine. We just
recognized one another and would be able to find each other, even
if lost amidst the jumbled mass of wandering humanity.

"Where do you live?"

"It's a long way from here."

I asked him once, and that was it, never again. I was afraid to
ask again, just as I was afraid to look at him. I'd be tortured with
apprehension and would tell myself, "What if he doesn't even have
a house, so what? You can't build a house on the waves of the
sea."

Whenever a twinkling star rose up into the skies to take its
place, he would stand near the window and look at the star as
though he were standing on the deck of a ship, the sea stormy and
the night dark, trying to find his way, almost like looking for a
landmark, a landmark of life. Then he would sigh and go over to
put on his boots. And if I would ask, "You'll telephone?," he'd say,
"I can't call from the middle of the ocean, and you don't have a
wireless..."

But this time, as he was leaving, I asked, "When are you coming back?" I had never said this before and he looked pensive. He
then turned around and pointed to the calligraphic design he had
drawn for me one day. "When the seas catch fire."

It made me turn cold and a painful tremor shot up my spine. I
think he realized this and changed the subject again: "It's a pity to
waste this flowerpot. Plant something in it, something you like."

And he left.

For a while I could hear his footsteps and then the splashing of
the water as he dove in to the sea, could hear how his hands
picked the seaweed at the bottom of the sea, or the coral...

My house was filled with the things he always brought me...
Colored seashells in which the stormy seas roared day and night,
shellfish, starfish and branches of coral...

How did I become acquainted with him, when and where?

It's useless to say that words make everything sound like a
business memo. Everyone knows this, but I also know that you
have to recall a memory once in a while, a memory that was a part
of your life in times long ago, before your earthly body took form
and began to move through space. It's as though there's an outer

surface and, one day a person remembers this memory while on this earthly plane and, if you are alert and perceptive, you will recognize it when you see it and penetrate through the surface to the interior.

The first time I saw him was on a bored afternoon. I was sitting on the boulders looking at the sea, a combination of green, blue and gray...my heart could not give them up, Bushire and the sea. I had come from Tehran and would come to sit on the boulders every afternoon at sunset.

That particular day I saw that someone else was there too, someone in a white naval uniform, just standing there, almost as if listening intently to something, listening in the direction of the sea.

It seemed he was wrestling with a problem as he slowly came towards me, doffed his hat and said, "Do you hear it, too?"

When he sat next to me, the sun was sunken halfway into the water and we were already close friends, knowing each other well, though he didn't seem all that familiar with the sea. He had recently been commissioned and now was obliged to start a life on the sea.

I said, "It's the sound of seashells..."

"Ah...." And the seashells were calling "whoow...ooow..." and you could hear the sounds of the starfish twinkling and the branches of coral petrifying. "Is it always like this?" he asked. "Always at sunset?"

"No," I replied, "only when something's happening."

"What is it?," he asked.

I said nothing until the shellfish gingerly poked out of their shells and started climbing up my hands and feet. "One of the mermaids must be lonely. You know that the mermaids fall in love while they are aquatic, and one of them must have fallen for a fisherman or, maybe a sailor...I'm going, I'm definitely going. It's quite unusual for them to call out from the middle of the ocean, from the blue-green depths...." He laughed silently. He was quiet, the sea murmuring, the shellfish wailing...

I remember his laugh, a laugh which, with each passing day, becomes clearer in some aspect or another. Maybe he knew everything and was laughing at me, maybe he was surprised, or maybe his laugh was the laughter of exile, the laugh of a seafaring man who had wound up on dry land.

We went together, me and him, in his white naval uniform, and the shellfish, some big and some tiny and the sea creatures which wrapped around our arms and legs, and the weeping starfish curling their colorful arms.

We went along until one of the mermaids began trembling with mortal fever. There was tar at the roots of her watery hair, and her body smelled of oil. She rasped with each breath. Her eyes were half-open and you couldn't look at her, for if you looked and saw those half-opened, oil-bleared eyes, you'd burst out sobbing and you couldn't....

The smell of oil permeated everything and the memory of the sea was gradually fading from the minds of the mermaids. They were trembling and turning red before my eyes and those of the young sailor.

I said, "My God, do you see what's happening? From now on the sea is always stormy. The mermaids are turning red with rage. The sea is dark forever more; the moon comes to play with the mermaids and now look, see for yourself...."

He was silent, looking at one of the feverish mermaids with tar stuck in the roots of her hair and her body smelling of oil.

Crying, I said, "This is the work of the sharks; the sharks have done this." I cried till morning and when we came ashore from the water and the sun rose, we were sitting on the boulders and I was still crying and he was deep in thought. He was afraid of the mermaids when they cried.

I had said that the weeping of mermaids makes the oceans rise, so much so that the port, the port of Bushire, would drown. He was thinking and sighing and there was something in the depths of his eyes that made it impossible for me to look at him, just like the last time he had said in this very house, "Plant something in your flowerpot, something you like..."

When the incident was about to pass, at that very moment I was here, in Tehran, in this very apartment—number 40, on the fourth floor, above Qaytariyeh Park...The building was swaying, like a ship rolling on the sea, the walls were giving way, like a ship being hit by laser-guided missiles. The flowerpots were shaking, the picture frames on the walls were falling and I heard screaming, strange screams, and I knew that the sharks are swallowing the sea, bringing about a general holocaust. Neither the radio nor the television said anything about it. Such words, by the time they reach me, are dying and their corpses fall all around me. They always smell, the corpses of dead and decaying words, words that have struggled for years and years to reach me, but never made it.

The news reached me in a different way, when the waters rose to just below my window on the fourth floor. When the shellfish and the starfish, weeping, reached me, I could hear an unearthly roar. I know how the shouting of earth people sounds, it is dusty and prolonged, black, smelling of the must of history, like a wild destructive cyclone. This wailing was the wailing of sea creatures, the cry of seabirds, a cry filled with pain and pure crystal sorrow, behind which you could see the moon reddening and darkening.

Whoow...oooow

I got up and closed the curtains. The water was rising everywhere. The green sea water and the trees of Qaytariyeh Park were drowning and the shellfish were coming through the cracks in the windowframe and crawling up the walls of my house.

And then, when I saw her, the mermaid that had grown wan and whose eyes had sunken in from over-crying and whose watery body had been lacerated by laser beams...I realized that it was true and that everything had happened as it must. I reached out beyond the railing on the balcony and, with the waves of the sea splashing in my face, I found it hard to breathe. The waves of the sea were washing over the roof, but despite this I grabbed hold of the mermaid, so thin and gasping for air. She sat on this black sofa, the same one upon which a young sailor had once sat, she sat and cried.

It seems the sea had caught fire. The shellfish and the coral and the mermaids all wailed in mourning in my house and the seabirds flew above the city with their anguished cries. And I wanted to see him, his childlike smile, his big lemon-shaped eyes, his taut, wan cheeks and his straight hair which he would sometimes push back from his forehead with his hand. But where was he?

The fish, which were, after all, fish, with breath that smelled like fish, were, large and small, coming through the cracks in the doors and windows, up the steps...The marsh palm in the flowerpot was bobbing on the water, shorn of its withered fronds. And then I saw, with my own eyes, a frantic little fish fix his eyes, big lemon-shaped eyes that were always staring at the stars, the twinkling stars, on the flowerpot.

When the waters receded, the mermaid grew calm and went off to grow old with her sorrow, and there was left only me and the big clay, dirty flowerpot, which smelled like the salt of the sea, a sea full of sharks, sharks that also roamed the earth.

Spring 1988

Shahlâ Shafiq (Her name appears as Chahla Chafiq in French sources) has chosen the pen name Shafiq in honor of her mother, Shafiqeh ("compassionate"). She works in a research institute in Paris and is completing her Ph.D. dissertation, a sociological study of the lives of Muslim women who have immigrated to the West. She has participated in research projects studying the role of immigrant women as cultural mediators in France and the lives of emigré women from Morocco and Turkey, both in their own countries and in the countries to which they have immigrated. She has published two books in French on Islam and Iranian women: *La Femme et le retour de l'Islam: l'expérience irannienne* (Paris: Éditions du Félin, 1991) [*Woman and the Return to Islam: The Iranian Experience*] and, in conjunction with Farhad Khosrow-Khavar, *Les femmes sous le voile, face a la loi Islamique* [*Women Under the Veil, in the Face of Islamic Law*], which was published in April 1995.

In addition to these academic studies, Shahla Shafiq has also explored the lives of Iranian women through fiction. She has written several short stories in Persian which have been published in periodicals such as *Nimeh-ye digar* (*The Other Half*), *Cheshmandâz* (*Perspective*), and *Afsâneh* (*Myth*).

The story selected here, "*The Wall*" ("*Divâr*," published in *Chashmandâz*, no. 11, pp. 116-118, Winter, 1993), depicts the experience of two women, leftists protesting in favor of the Revolution, who are cornered by an angry mob of religious demontrators, whose Islamic understanding of the meaning of the Iranian Revolution is quite at odds with theirs.

8

The Wall
Shahla Shafiq

The voice coming over the loudspeaker said, "Comrades, we'll end the demonstration with the slogan 'Death to the reactionaries, long live the Revolution' and then we'll disperse."

There were no *Hezbullahi*s around. The feverish sense of anticipation, which had reached new heights with each successive slogan, gave way to a quiet joy. A muffled clamor rose from the crowd and the regiment of demonstrators divided up into small groups and spilled out into the streets around Fowzieh Square.

I found Farzaneh in the crowd, which was steadily shrinking, and we set off, talking together, toward the sidewalk across the street. We didn't want to leave just yet; sensing an emptiness, we searched people's faces for signs of the effect of our slogans. The autumn sunset was quickly succumbing to the dreary darkness as night descended from the skies and spread out through the streets. Farzaneh said, "There's nothing happening. Let's cross the street and catch a cab."

All of a sudden, we both realized that we couldn't go anywhere. There were people coming towards us in groups of two or three, from behind, from in front and on both sides. The way they were approaching us, it was clear we could not change direction; no matter which direction we went, we would be cut off. Farzaneh said, "Good grief, they're coming right at us" and pulled the knot of her head kerchief tighter. I said, "We'd better stay calm and keep on walking."

Now they were coming together. We could no longer see the street; we had been surrounded by a human wall. The shutters of the shops beside us were closing one by one, with a deafening clatter. Farzaneh said, "They're not gonna let us in," and put her hand on her stomach. I thought she was going to throw up. In step with us the human wall moved along with a muffled commotion, veering this way and that. It seemed about to collapse on us at any moment. Eyes, like dark holes in a wall, stared out from among them, gazes fiery and fixed. The mouth cavities were opening and closing, emitting incomprehensible, broken sounds. Somebody shouted, "God is great." The mouths opened all at the same time, like a gaping pit from which the cry "God is great" reverberated. Hands were being thrust into the air, clenched in fists, and falling back down, unclenched. They came out of the wall like hooks and once again disappeared into it. Cracks opened in the wall, hundreds of them, one after the other, and the wall would part only to come together once again. It rumbled with their breathing and shouting, moving closer.

I felt a tugging at my kerchief from behind: "Hey, you sluts!... Is this any way to wear your kerchiefs!! You tryin' to bring shame on us?"

Farzaneh softly whispered in my ear, "I'm pregnant." I thought, "Poor thing! It's hard to tell by looking at her belly. She must be in her first months." She was clinging to me so tightly that I thought I could hear the fetus's pulse beating fearfully in her womb. "Don't look at them," she said under her breath.

I felt that just by looking at them, we would be sucked into that dark pit and devoured. We were looking down and it seemed as if we were sinking deeper and deeper into a black boiling, oozing tar of insults, shouts, laughing and panting. I felt it was not possible to take one more step, that the wall would crash down on our heads at any instant. I pictured all those heavy men's shoes kicking Farzaneh in the stomach and saw my own body in their voracious, hook-like hands.

Farzaneh's sweaty hands firmly grabbed my wrist and dragged me with her. A door opened behind us. The screech of the metal shutters of the shop as they closed mingled with the crescendo of shouts outside. We were in a room with two desks and a few chairs — a small office. Farzaneh sat on the first chair, her sweaty blond hair stuck to her forehead. Her eyes were turning red. Facing towards the owner of the establishment, she said, "Thank you very much, sir." I repeated her words, "Really, thank you very, very much." The man was chubby and middle-aged. He picked up the phone receiver: "I'll take care of it. These people are rivaled only by their own kind. I'll call the *Komiteh* to come...."

The shop's shutters shook with their cries: "Let them out... They've got grenades in their purses... God is great...Death to the unveiled....Death to the anti-revolutionaries..."

Farzaneh said, "I'll call Mohsen to come and get us; it's better..." She asked the shop owner if she could use his phone.

As soon as Farzaneh hung up the phone, the man said, "I have to open the shop; otherwise, they'll pull the shutter off its hinges and break down the door...."

I said, "Excuse me, sir. This lady is with child..." He looked at us with sympathy, "You see...I've no choice."

As the shutter went up, the noise of the crowd intensified. A number of people in the crowd applauded. The door opened and a hot blast of noise and breath struck us in the face. My hand trembled in Farzaneh's hands and my knees had grown weak. A row of hands with fingers interlocked formed a chain holding back the swarming crowd. The crowd pushed forward against the chain of hands, which threatened to break at any moment. In a loud voice the owner of the shop said, "Brothers, I've called the *Komiteh* to come. Calm down." Someone in the chain shouted, "The *Komiteh* is on its way. Back up." Farzaneh whispered, "Our own buddies are in the chain."

The crowd seethed forward, wanting to break the barrier. The pits of their mouths were growing wider and deeper. Somebody in the front row shouted, "Hands off, brothers! Hands off!...The *Komiteh* is on its way." As I raised my head, I saw a familiar face. It was Behrooz, my classmate at the college. His hands were locked firmly in the grasp of the person standing beside him. Beads of sweat were quivering on his anxious temples. His eyes, stubborn and worried, watched over the bending chain of hands.

When the *Komiteh* members arrived, the crowd drew back, annoyed. They didn't want to leave. The crowd stood poised, snorting softly, like a hungry beast waiting to be fed. Behrooz came out of the front row and told the head of the *Komiteh* members that he had witnessed the course of events from the beginning. He was ready to go to the *Komiteh* to testify that we were busy shopping and the crowd had mistaken us. At that moment, Mohsen arrived and told the leader of the *Komiteh* members that his wife was with child and that he had to take her to the doctor. The *Komiteh* members whispered to each other. Their leader finally turned towards the crowd and shouted, "Brothers, break it up." Dissatisfied, the crowd milled about, hesitating. Grumbling, they finally dispersed. They stood around in small groups here and there, watching. A few of them followed us to the bus stop.

It was after Farzaneh and Mohsen got off the bus that my whole body began to ache with pain and fear. It seemed as if those pits were becoming one big mouth, spitting all of their rage and contempt into my face. Those dark holes now became one eye socket, filled with a fiery stare. Those hands, those shameless hands were groping over my body, inflicting pain and disgrace upon me. I laid my head on the arm of the seat; my whole body was convulsed by pitiful sobbing.

Someone sat next to me. It was Behrooz: "I didn't want them to know I knew you, or I would have come with you. Do you feel OK?"

He had a worried look on his face. His hands were there, beside me — without molesting me. They were large hands, full of affectionate veins. Instinctively, I reached for them and took them firmly in my hands. Embarrassed, Behrooz sat up straight in his seat. I would have dearly liked to put my head on his shoulder. How I wished he would hold me. I longed for the safety of his compassionate hands. He looked at me in confusion and edged away from me in his seat.

Royâ Shâpuriân was born in Tehran in 1966 and studied medicine at the University of Tehran. She wrote several short stories while still a student, dealing with the hospital environment and the psychological state of patients, including the 1986 story *"Niyâz"* (*"Need"*), which won critical recognition. She also treats the clash of modern and traditional conceptions about family relationships and women's issues in Iran.

The first story by Shâpuriân, *"Dark Eyes, Shining Stars"* (*"Yek chashm-e siâh, yek setâreh-ye rowshan"*), published in *Dâstânhâ-ye kutâh az nevisandegân-e Irân va jahân*, edited by Safdar Taqizâdeh and Asghar Elâhi (Tehran: Enteshârât-e `Elmi, 1991, pp. 217-222), deals with a young woman's hopes and fears, a girl imagining her ideal beloved as hopeful suitors come to call at her home, first for her older sister and then for herself.

The second story, *"Shrivelled Petals"* (*"Golbarghâ-ye palâsideh"*), appeared in a well-known Iranian woman's journal (*Zanân* 7, Fall 1992, pp. 30-32), and delicately portrays the anxieties of a young woman diagnosed with breast cancer.

9

Dark Eyes, Shining Stars

Roya Shapurian

I can hear no more talking, not even whispering. All the madness has died down and regret has taken its place. I am thinking about life tonight, just like I do every night, but I am not counting the stars. They are so dim that beauty cannot reveal through them its grandeur. I am thinking that dark eyes can shine brighter and illumine other skies better than the stars.

I am staring at my eyes in the mirror and I would dearly like for them to shine a little. First, I look at all those present in the room. Then I look down and sit in the corner like a good girl. Immediately mother tells me, "Mehri, dear, would you bring us tea?," so she can begin enumerating my talents. She doesn't let me sit there even for a minute to figure out what is going on, but praises the visitors effusively when they are gone and says that they were marvelous people.

I don't like to mess with my eyes. When I put black eyeliner on, they no longer look at anything affectionately. But mother says, "After all, it simply won't do not to add a touch of makeup here and there."

Mahin said, "They look you over from head to toe. They stare at you so hard you think there's something wrong with you, or your dress is askance or something. But every time you turn around and look at yourself in the mirror, you see that you are your regular old self, only more helpless."

Mahin was so worried that she could not sit still. She was constantly fidgeting, as though she was about to get up and do something. She would say, behind my back, "How many more times, then?"

I know that I will finally find you even if I have to go to the ends of the earth, for you are the one, though still a stranger. You are the one calling me from the outer reaches of your loneliness, expecting only a kind word from me. Your eyes are not bright enough to see my beauty, but you always have an answer for me every time my voice chokes with sorrow.

I go to the closet, open the door and size up each and every dress. How about the red blouse with the dark skirt?! But, no, a red blouse wouldn't be appropriate for the first meeting. It may not be dignified... I'll wear the white shirt... No, they may say she's just dying to wear bridal white...Then, I should wear the black skirt with the blue blouse... Isn't it too conservative? I hope it won't look like I'm in mourning.

I told Mahin, "Wear your green blouse."

She said, "Isn't it a bit too sheer?"

I said, "How many times have you worn it?"

She said, "A few times here and there, but not on special occasions like this."

I said, "It doesn't matter. Don't worry about it."

She said, "Oh, I don't care any more." Then, she looked into my eyes and said, "Mother says that it'll get too late if you dilly dally." She paused for awhile and said, "I know that I won't be able to sleep again, thinking about the beginning of a new life, however ridiculous it may be."

I dreamed that you had offered your eyes to my soul and the images of this person and that would no longer pass across your gaze, not even for a moment. And you would like me and choose me without comparing me to others. I know that you will recognize me from my voice and my voice, which comes from within me, will be the only thing you love—not my smile, which I might have to cast before this or that person every now and then; not my tears, which I would not want you to see, unless they are tears of joy.

I take a plain off-white skirt out of the closet. I plug in the iron to warm it up and stare at its light. I am thinking it will light up whenever it is ready. The iron seems to know when the time comes, only we don't... As I press it over the skirt, I think it will never be as smooth as it should be to please all those present in the room.

Mahin said, "I hate it, just tell me how many more times I have to do it! They leave and never even call. Even if they come back, there will be an argument over the amount of gold and the dowry and it will end up with the two families no longer on speaking terms. Just like Auntie! They were in a store buying the things for the wedding, and her suitor just disappeared and never came back! Just the sort of people that we would get stuck with! Well, then, loneliness, old age and so much headache! But why must it be so?"

I am certain that your world is a different world, where the rainbow lives on after the rain and the sky is always blue. Where the daylight of the cloudless sky is never overtaken by night.

I unplug the iron and I hope that today will pass uneventfully, like every other day. I try to guess what his face would be like sitting across the room from me watching all of my movements.

Mahin was talking: "Do you remember the one who kept staring at me the entire time without even lowering his gaze once? When he went to take sugar cubes for his tea, you'd think he was carefully selecting them. And he wasn't satisfied with one or two cubes, either; he wanted five or six. Finally, I pulled the sugar bowl out of his reach."

At that point, she got up, paced around the room for awhile and said, "Walk into the room, go straight towards them, say 'hello' and come back immediately. Don't say another word. Stay behind the door and wait to see what will happen. One person is never enough to make the decision; he's got to bring Auntie dear, on his mother's side, along with him, and the Aunt on his father's side of the family, and Father and Grandpa, too!"

I smiled and said, "And, if I'm lucky, their brothers."

Mahin seemed to be exhausted. She was standing in front of the mirror, cleaning her face with a cotton ball. She said, "You're still a kid."

I wish I were a kid, but I am not. Everyone was saying, "As soon as you decide, you'll be a perfect housewife."

"Then, what about my school?"

"It's no good if you age; untimely wrinkles will ruin your face. What a pity if they should ruin you."

At first, I thought they were not serious, but eventually I realized that it would be best if I take a picture showing me in the bloom of youth and frame it—a picture that would never wrinkle, would never get angry, would not make demands, wouldn't burst into tears and wouldn't study.

My dream revolves all around those eyes of yours, in which there is no light. You do not know the color of my complexion, the wrinkles of my face do not bother you and, in your eyes, I never change and you always want me, only me.

When Mahin left, mother said, "You're the only one left."

And Uncle praised my mother, his sister, for having been able to marry off Mahin so successfully. I looked at myself in the mirror for hours, but I found nothing remarkable about myself, even though everyone had told me that night, "You look so pretty." I did not know what I would gain from that beauty and which part of my life would be filled by it, especially when I remembered that I was getting old... I did not think that I could submit to a simple choice just to escape growing old.

"May Mahin's good fortune take you under its wing!"

I said to myself that if Mahin's fortune was so omnipotent, it would have done something to help Mahin. When they were taking her away, her eyes had filled with tears, and I heard her mother-in-law tell her, "It isn't customary where we come from for the bride to cry. It's not a good omen!"

And I thought about the traditions and rituals which Mahin would henceforth have to perform or to avoid. And I would have loved to know at what time it is customary for one to burst into tears and how many times a day one could smile. Surely, the tradition in every provincial town is different, and a young lonely girl who becomes a member of a strange new family must be familiar with all of them. Otherwise, she will make an unforgivable mistake.

My mother was the last one to bid farewell to Mahin. She told her, "Kerman is a nice city, too. Its sky is full of stars."

I raised my hands to pray for her, but Mahin is no longer here to wish me luck today. I enter calmly. I greet everyone. I smile and offer them tea and let them look me over, either to select or reject me. But only if they let me keep my eyes for myself, with no makeup on them at all.

I think a pair of dark eyes can always shine brighter and illumine other skies better than the stars. I stretch my hands towards you and I know that only you can show the world to me. I have faith in your eyes and in what you know in the realms beyond everything worth seeing. Offer me your eyes and your world, in which there is no color.[7]

---

[7] There is an echo of poems by Ahmad Shâmlu, Iran's premier living poet, in these lines of the story. The two poems that come to mind are "Everyone's Love," which includes the lines: Tell me your name/give me your hand/speak to me/give me your heart/; and the other, "The Inner Chill," which is punctuated by the recurring line - O love, love/your blue visage cannot be seen.../your rose visage cannot be seen.../your familiar color cannot be seen....

10

Shrivelled Petals

Roya Shapurian

I was looking in the display window of the store. Hanging on the wall in the display area was a clock, its numbers carved from wood and its hands made out of stone. I thought to myself that stone hands would move rather slowly. I wanted to have it. Below it was a desk calendar with a marble frame and little white sheets of paper, on each of which was printed an aphorism:

> That which cannot be replaced, ye who are wise,
> is precious life: Know, then, its value.

I had been staring at the sheets of paper in the calendar, as they flipped by. The doctor was sitting behind his desk, playing with the calendar with his large hands, covered with coarse black hair. He was trying to pin down a date for the surgery. He must have known how many leaves of paper were left until the end of the year. He must have had calendars for several years into the future in his drawer, which he could flip through one by one, giving assurance to all that they needn't worry, that they would still be alive. As he came out of the room, he yelled behind me, "For now, go on a trip or something, anything to improve your state of mind."

I looked at the sculptures, all of which had a name: The flower-girl, the dishevelled date-tree, the laughing duck. My eye caught sight of the sculpture of the two horses. Two white horses were standing on a single pedestal, though it seemed they were neighing and galloping.

I said, "The one with the longer mane is me."

Javad replied, "No, he is more sprightly and stronger, so it must be me."

Now I have to tell him. "Javad, one of the horses got broken." I am sure he will frown and give me a look that will make me fade and blur. Now he's got to brush his mane forward and drape it over his shoulder to hide the crack. Then the one with the longer mane is me.

The doctor said, "The cost of the operation will not be so high. Don't worry. I'll talk with your husband."

I nodded. The knot in my throat made it hard to breathe.

"I don't know why people are so sensitive about some parts of their body," he said. "Now if I had said that I have to remove three-fourths of your liver, you wouldn't have given it another thought. But since it's your breast, you've got yourself all worked up about it."

A white dove flew into the air from the branch and a little boy with an orange hat and green workman's overalls was feeding seeds to the birds. The shop's owner had come over to the window and was looking at me. He was a friend of Javad's. They had made an agreement between themselves that whenever they visited each other's house, if either of them had a craving for anything, they would have it prepared right away. The last time he came to our house, he felt like *fesenjân*. My hands were black for a whole week afterwards because of the walnut shells.

In front of the door of a house, a man was standing in his pajamas, watering the flower bed alongside the street. The pressure of the water from the hose was so high I felt it would crush the flowers and make them droop. I reached the telephone booth. I thought I had better tell Javad over the phone. It would be easier that way; he wouldn't give me that look and I wouldn't get all flustered. I tell myself, "Now I've got to make a decision." I need a little peace and quiet. There were three people in line waiting for the phone. A man with a grubby felt hat on his head and a basketful of fresh hot bread was first in line. How about if I tell Javad to come here right now? We can go for a little walk, have a sandwich and go home. He might not feel like it, but well, it won't hurt to spend one little evening out of the house.

"Javad, I've been to the doctor."

"Well?"

He always tells me don't beat around the bush, get straight to the point. Don't waste time. But let him wait for me to do things at my own speed, this once. "Javad, I passed by the sculpture gallery," I tell him. "The two horses were still next to each other, neighing and galloping off. They were strong."

The doctor had said, "Don't be afraid at all. Many people are in the same situation. You are an intelligent woman; you have to weigh the matter carefully, as if in a balance. On the one hand, you can remove your breast and get on comfortably with your life. On the other hand, it could turn into a tumor, spread to your lungs, cause you difficulty in breathing and ruin your life."

Mother was sitting on the hospital bed, staring at me with fixed eyes. Even when she closed her eyes, her stare remained impressed upon your being. I was pacing around her bed, moving the flowers that they had brought her, throwing out the shrivelled petals, changing the water in the vase. The doctor said to raise the head of the bed so that she could breathe easier. When she would lay down, she couldn't breathe anymore.

The little boy behind me said, "Go ahead. It's your turn."

I told him, "No, you make your call. Your mother must be worried about you. I'll go to the next booth."

A little girl and her mother were coming towards me. She was pulling on her mother's arm. "If you don't buy me a ball, I won't come home with you." Her mother was young and her face was thickly made-up. The swell of her breasts was clearly visible underneath her overcoat. I passed by an ice cream parlor. Traditional Iranian ice cream, Italian ice, *fáludeh*, fruit juice.

I went in. "Sir, give me a traditional Iranian ice cream."

He was about to put the change in my hand. I pulled my hand back so he would put it on the table. The first spoonful I put in my mouth was so cold it burned my throat.

"Ma'am, there is a chair here. Have a seat."

Two soldiers were sharing a table, and the table next to them was empty. Before sitting down, my foot caught on the table leg and I almost fell. One of them said, "She didn't know there were two of us, or she would have brought a girlfriend."

I put down my purse and settled myself into the chair. I would have liked to take the mirror out of my purse and look at my face, but couldn't.

The soldier with the henna-colored moustache said to the other one, "I've been thinking I might go to one of the provinces, like Kazerun, or somewhere. It would decrease the length of my military service."

"There's less than six months of service left for me. You're just at the beginning; you better come up with a more substantial plan. Go get a Commission of Military Service form. Work something out for yourself."

"My father says until you do your military service, you're not a man."

I took another spoonful of ice cream and put it in my mouth. I crushed the cream with my teeth and swallowed.

I asked the doctor, "Will it affect my ability to have children?"

"There's nothing to be worried about. You're young and you will be as good as new after you beat the disease."

The woman in the bed next to mother's in the hospital had brown raised spots all over her body. At first they thought it was leprosy and her husband went and divorced her in absentia. Then they discovered it was some curable skin disease. She would always point out the iron beams of the ceiling in the room and count them. She'd say, "That's as many as the children I've had. They've given them all to my husband." An old man with a cane came into the ice cream parlor. He cracked a joke for the shop owner and smiled a smile as wide as his face. The man set a glass of *fâludeh* in front of him. He picked it up and went on his way. When he passed by me he said, "I wanted to be your lover, but my mamma didn't let me."

I wanted to get up, but my ice cream wasn't finished. The soldier behind me was still talking animatedly. "The best of all is being crippled. Go cut off one of your legs and you'll be released from service. Then you can get an artificial leg. In exchange, you'll have stolen back two years of your life, which will be all yours. In fact, did you know they'll excuse you from service if your stomach is missing? Let's see now, can you block up that worthless stomach of yours? Go and tell them, 'Sir, I am ill, I am a weakling. Have mercy on me. My head is empty, my hands are empty, my stomach is empty.'" And he laughed uproariously.

I pictured the other one sitting across from him, his eyes fixed on his friend's mouth, trying to figure out what to do with his life. My spoon had reached the bottom of the dish—the ice cream had melted and was sliding off the spoon, but I couldn't let it go to waste.

If I were at home, I would have slurped the rest of it down. As I got up, my head felt dizzy. I saw the scales the doctor had mentioned teetering up and down in front of my eyes. Pain and weakness and exhaustion, or a simple operation? I had to make a decision.

As I was leaving the ice cream parlor, the owner said, "Please come again." Behind him was a flowerpot with three stalks of gladiolas, with several long stems on each—from which grew a few not yet opened buds. I thought that if he would prune the wilted petals, the buds would open up quicker and blossom.

Tâhereh Alavi was born in Tehran on 17 December 1959. After finishing high school, she began working at the Bureau of Child and Youth Education (Kânun-e Parvaresh-e Kudakân va Nownahâlân). She went to France in 1986 to pursue an education in children's literature and lived there for six years editing and translating literary works for children and teenagers into Persian. She has also produced a number of works for adults, including a collection of her own short stories, entitled *In Memory of the Little House* (*Be yâd-e khâne-ye kuchek*) and a number of translations from French into Persian, including the popular 1878 novel, *Sans famille*, by the children's writer Hetor Malot (1830-1907), as well as works by Henri Bosco (1888-1976) and the Mexican author, Jose Vasconcelos (1882-1959). Ms. Alavi is a regular contributor to Persian periodicals, such as *Negâh-e Now* (*A New Vision*), *Kiân* (*Saturn*) and *Zanân* (*Women*). She currently lives in Tehran.

This story, *"Counting"* (*"Shomaresh"*, from the magazine *Zanân*, vol. 3, no. 20, Tehran, 1994, pp. 26-7), illustrates the minute thoughts and worries of a young, neglected Iranian wife, whose hair is falling out.

11

Counting
Tahereh Alavi

I sit on the chair, pick up the comb and comb my hair. My hair is black as night and short as the hours of sleep. As the comb reaches the end of my hair, I start again—from top to bottom, from back to front, once, ten times, a hundred times. This is the best way. The doctor has said that I should comb my hair very hard a hundred times a night to get the blood under my scalp circulating; maybe it will stop falling out. But I'm losing more hair, which I arrange neatly in a row on my dressing-table and count. I get tired and stop counting. The doctor says that I should stop counting because it causes me more anxiety which will cause more hair to fall out. Every night more than the last. A hundred, a hundred and ten, a hundred and twenty, a hundred and...

But I can't stop looking at them. The number of dead hairs tells how the day went. If the number is large, it means it was a hard day; and if it was a hard day, the number will definitely be large.

I see my husband in the mirror walking towards his desk. He sits at the desk, picks up a pen and takes out some paper. How he loves his work! I know. I love him, too, but I am not sure whether he knows. I open my mouth to tell him once more; my voice rattles in my throat but doesn't come out. Or maybe the sound does come out, but my husband can't hear it. I try one more time; I open my mouth, but quickly change my mind and begin combing again. A hundred twenty, a hundred thirty, a hundred and...

The loss of hair has eighty-seven (or was it seventy-eight?) causes, only a few of which have been discovered: malnutrition, bacterial diseases, sudden loss of weight and neurological disorders. But I am a calm person; my husband says so. I know that in order to do his work, he needs peace and quiet—a quiet neighborhood, a quiet house and a quiet wife.

It is natural for hair to fall out, between sixty and a hundred strands a day. The doctor says, "Eat well and sleep well." In order to fall asleep, I count the stars: One star, two stars, three stars....My eyes light upon the dressing-table and the row of hairs, and I continue counting: four hairs, five hairs, six hairs....

The day before yesterday, a friend of mine jokingly said, "Are you building an expressway on your scalp?"

She was right; the loss of hair reveals progressively more scalp. My husband roared with laughter. It was a long time since I had seen him laugh. His laughter made me laugh, too; I laughed a lot. Nevertheless, that night I counted one hundred forty-five strands of dead hair.

I'm not going to count my hair any more; I have made up my mind. I get up to walk around the house. My husband is hard at work. How fast the words flow from the nib of his pen. I go over to him. I want to touch his curly hair, but am afraid the words would be startled and flee from his memory. I just stand next to him for a while, but he is completely oblivious. As he says, "When I'm busy working, my mind is in another world." I return to the mirror. I want to reach out and sweep away all those pieces of hair on the dressing-table, but I don't. Counting them keeps me busy and occupies my mind. A hundred forty, a hundred fifty, a hundred....

The dead hairs remind me of dead people, dead people remind me of dead mothers, and dead mothers remind me of my own mother, who is not yet dead. But it has been a long time since she visited our house, and how badly I miss her!

The chair squeaks and I suddenly come to myself. I quickly wipe the tears off my face. I know that my husband doesn't like me crying. All artists are like that; they are sensitive people whose feelings are upset and disturbed by even the slightest things. This is what my husband says, and I believe him. I believe everything he tells me. That's what my mother says. Before I get a chance to collect myself, or at least straighten up the pieces of hair laid out on the dressing-table, I see my husband standing over me. The comb slides slowly through my fingers and falls on the floor at my feet. Thank God that he doesn't notice it. I ask, "Did you win or lose?" He doesn't answer, he just smiles. I know that he is a winner. He has always been a winner. For a moment, he holds my hand in his and then lies down on the bed. A while later, when he gets up, I am still tired and worn out, crumpled up in a corner of the bed, my eyes closed, following the shuffle of his slippers. He stands at the dressing-table for a moment. This time he sees the strands of my hair. He casts a glance at me, sneers and goes away. One must be hard-hearted to laugh at the dead; even so, he is a poet. A few moments later, I hear the sound of the toilet being flushed and once again I squeeze the comb hard between my fingers:

A hundred sixty, a hundred seventy, a hundred....

Soudâbeh Ashrafi was born in Iran on 12 December 1959 and has been living in the United States since 1985. She began her career as a writer in 1990 and since then has published several short stories in Persian literary periodicals both inside and outside Iran, including *Simorgh, Gardun, Donyâ-ye sokhan, Fâkhteh, Kurosh* and *Kelk.* She has also translated a few stories and interviews. She lives in Irvine, California and her collection of stories entitled *Fire in the Wheat Field* (*Âtash dar gandom-zâr*) is currently in press in Iran.

The story, *"The Loom"* (*"Dâr-e qâli,"* published in *Simorgh,* no. 18, Mission Viejo, CA, February/March 1993, pp. 76-77), is a condemnation of the exploitation of girls and women by the carpet industry, and by their own relatives.

12

The Loom
Soudabeh Ashrafi

The noonday summer sun was shining. Gohar was spreading the clothes on the clothesline stretched from one side of the courtyard to the other, when her father, with a bag under his arm, came in. Gohar thought, "He's going to start now."

"Girl, come and take these!" She took the bag and emptied the apples into the pond. The fish hastily dove to the bottom of the pond, and the apples floated on the water. "He's going to ask about Mom now; he's going to make a dupe of her again..."

"What's the matter with you? Why the wrinkled brow?

"Nothing's the matter, Sir."

Father took the jacket off his shoulders and wiped the sweat off his forehead. "On the way home I saw Nasrollah Khan's son. What a fine young man! God preserve him!"

Gohar collected the apples floating on the water. Father bent his head, passed under the clotheslines and stood in the shade of the corner of the wall. Gohar looked at her long shadow through the corner of her eyes.

"When he started out, he was just a simple worker. Now, God watch over him, he's become a technician! Got a raise, bonus, clothing, food supplies... every month... Yes, siree! He's made something of himself at the old armory... If he gets married, they'll give 'em an apartment to live in....So where's your mother, then?

Don't tell me she's been kidnapped by an elf?" He wanted to joke. Gohar was still standing with her back to him; she did not see the trace of a smile on his face that quickly faded away. "She's been busy weaving the rug, Sir. She's not come downstairs since this morning."

Father entered the vestibule. The girl followed in his tracks, opening and closing her eyes to adjust to the dark. Father said, "It's nice and cool here. Lay the table spread right here. But close the courtyard gate; the strangers passing on the street can see us."

Gohar went out again, slammed the gate, passed through the vestibule and turned on the kitchen lamp under the stairs. Her eyes were still filled with sunlight. She thought, "I told him to buy a pair of glasses for her or she'd go blind. She overheard me and said, 'I told you that I don't want glasses. I'm too old for that.' She's ashamed to wear glasses. So Father said, 'Who says anybody bought you glasses?'" The smoke was rising from one side of the blue lamp with its three wicks.

Mother was sitting with her legs crossed on the plank, which was one meter off the ground, in front of the loom. The fingers of her right hand were clutching the white warp strings, and the knife, which she used to cut the threads, had slipped through her fingers and dropped into her lap. Her head was resting against the shed stick, which ran horizontally through the warp strings of the rug. The colorful balls of yarn were hanging against the surface of the suspended rug. Her black hair, long enough to reach her shoulders, was tied behind her head with a strip of white thread.

Father went straight to the clothes-peg. He reached for the buckle of his belt. "It's time for the noon prayer; leave off work." There was no answer.

"God willing, we'll set out tomorrow afternoon. My brother and Ahmad will come here first. You have a decent bedroll, right? We'll stay at the Port for a few days, then we'll hit the sea. We'll go to Dubai and around there. Ahmad says there are more jobs this year than last year, but undoubtedly there are more workers, too."

The sunbeam shining through the window made the tiny particles floating in the room much brighter. "Don't you think it would've been better to weave a two-cubit rug this time? They sell much better." He heard only his own voice. The woman's fingers still hung motionless, laced in the layers of white yarn. The room was not filled with the usual repetitive sound of cutting thread.

"On the way home, I saw Nasrollah Khan's son..." He couldn't take it anymore: "Have you gone deaf and dumb today? Why don't you answer me?"

There was still no other sound or movement in the room. Usually when the woman was busy weaving, the sound of the radio or her own soft whisper would fill the room. Her shoulders, arms, forearm and fingers would work harmoniously together, in simultaneous motion, and the knife blade hitting the threads would make a dull, monotonous noise. Then, as she reached the end of each row of the weft, would come the turning of the shed stick and heddle rod. She would weave the thin, dark blue thread through the white warp strings and then, her hands moving rhythmically up and down, she would pound down on the threads with her weaving comb, making sure the weft strings sat tightly in the warp.

"It's half past noon; get up, give us a bite for lunch." He went towards the loom and laid his hand on the woman's arm. The woman's fingers slipped out of the threads and her hand fell heavily on her lap. The man grabbed her shoulders, pulled her back and shouted, "Hey, Gohar! God damn you! Come here..."

Gohar dropped the plates on the floor and ran into the room. The woman's head, with her black hair, was held in her husband's hands, her body half suspended in the air and half resting on the plank in front of the loom.

"She's dead! Oh Dear God! Is she dead?"

"Go get a bowl of water for me to splash in her face. She'll come around. Go! I said, get a move on."

The woman's body was lying by the loom beside the heaps of fluffy colorful wool, the sunlight falling over her dress. Her face was calm and her eyes were closed. Gohar ran into the room with a bowl of water. She extended the bowl towards her father and looked at her mother's motionless body. "Let's take her to the doctor, Sir."

"Where to find a doctor now? Useless lot! Open her mouth.

She's fainted. Open it. I'll pour the water."

"Her feet have swollen, Sir."

"Don't get on my case. There's nothing wrong with her."

The woman, her eyelids still closed, was lying silently by the frame of the loom on which hung the rug, with its sky-blue medallion, as yet unfinished, on a field of crimson, dotted with small colorful flowers. The water they had poured into her mouth was spilling out the corners of her lips. Gohar turned her moist eyes to her father and asked plaintively, "Then, at least let me go get Naneh Ali."

At the end of the lane Naneh Ali had spit on the ground and, with the tip of her slippers, was covering over the wad with dirt. She shouted at the kids who were pitching pennies in the shade: "Don't you brats have someplace else to hang around? Git on home, all of you, beat it!"

Gohar, breathless, grabbed Naneh Ali's shoulders from behind: "Naneh Ali, Nan... Ali, come! Come and save my mother. She's fainted. My dad says she's f...fainted."

"Ok, my child! Don't panic. Go on, I'm right behind you."

The kids were still making faces at Naneh Ali and laughing.

"Let me go get the herbal medicine, child." When she returned, she held her cupped hands before Gohar's face. There was a small black box in them. "Search from one end of Tehran to the other, child, you won't find an herbal medicine like this." Gohar looked in the old woman's eyes, which had no eyelashes, and at her dried eyelids. She was no longer in a hurry. "Remember when your mother had a backache? The very same herbal medicine made her better....Dry cupping kills a backache, too."

*****

After the week of mourning was over, Haj Agha Varamini measured the rug and said, "Mashdi, it's of no value to me at all. I have to give it to a skilled weaver to finish the job. And it might not be much use even after that. What if it comes out crooked?..."

He stroked his beard with the palm of his hand. He bent over the rug and squinted at its design, rotating his rosary beads with both hands in a circle behind his back.

"But, Haj Agha! My daughter is a witness how much, God rest her soul, she sweated over this."

"What's the use, Mashdi? She's gone and she didn't finish it." He took his eyes off the rug, looked over at Gohar and said, "Mashdi, God preserve her! My how big your daughter has grown! Sit her at the loom. Even supposing she can't weave two-cubit rugs as nicely as her mother could, she can at least manage a thick-napped one."

Shokuh Mirzadegi was born in Tehran in 1945, and her first stories appeared in Iran in the periodical *Ferdowsi* in 1970. She has published two collections of short stories entitled *Constant Restlessness (Bi-qarâri-hâ-ye pâydâr)* and *Begin Again (Aghâz-i dovvom)*; a book of plays entitled *The Exiles of the Year 3000 (Tab`idihâ-ye sâl-i 3000)*, two collections of children's stories *Sunflower (Gol-e âftâb)* and *'Jik jik-i mastun'* as well as numerous research articles, including a book-length historical study of the status of women in Iran [*Sayr-e nozuli-e zan az âghâz tâ Eslâm*]. Living in exile, she has edited a number of Persian-language periodicals, including *Forbidden Things (Mamnu`eh-hâ)*, *Resistance (Moqâvemat)* and currently co-edits a quarterly journal, *Puyeshgarân (The Seekers)*, published in Denver, Colorado. While living in London, she published a political novel, *That Alien in Me (Bigâneh-'i dar man)*. She is currently working with her husband, Esmâ'il Nuri-'Alâ, on two books, *Imagery in Modern Persian Poetry (Imâzh dar she`r-e mo`âser-i Fârsi)* and *Literature and Art in the West in the Twentieth Century (Adabiyât va honar-e qarn-e bistom dar Gharb.)* She is also working on a forthcoming book entitled *Important Women in Iranian History (Zanân-e mohemm-e târikh-e Irân.)* Meanwhile, a further book of short stories, entitled *Golden Ark*, is in press (Sherkat-e ketâb, Los Angeles) and she is putting the finishing touches on a novel.

"The Young John" ("*Jân-e javân,*" published in *Puyeshgarân*, no. 5, May 1993, London, pp. 44-49) is about the friendship between two Iranian emigrés in England (where Shokuh Mirzadegi makes her home), and the conflicting impulses toward assimilation to one's new language and culture on the one hand, and the desire to preserve one's heritage, on the other.

The second story by Mirzadegi, "*Setareh in the Mist*", ("*Setareh dar meh,*" published in *Puyeshgarân*, nos. 8-9, June 1995, Denver, pp.16-24), is a morbid tale of a family driven into dire poverty by political circumstances that is forced to resort to prostitution to save itself. In the end, however, the husband is consumed by sexual jealousy and in a delusional state reminiscent of Sadeq Hedayat's *The Blind Owl*, murders his victimized wife.

13

The Young John
Shokuh Mirzadegi

A few men, dressed in black, are standing outside John's apartment, ready to carry his corpse to the cemetery; they are busy talking to an old man whom I have seen from time to time in the hallways. I think it is Michael. I say hello to the old man and, as always, he returns my greeting warmly and lets me in. As I pass by him, he whispers and says, "It's unbelievable! Unbelievable! John was feeling very well."

Most of the neighbors are present in the living room, with a few people whom I do not remember having seen anywhere. Maggie is sitting in a corner, right next to the big box, which must contain John's dead body; she is talking soberly. As soon as she sees me, she opens her arms and says, "Oh...Parvaneh! My dear friend! He loved you as if you were our own daughter."

As I nestle in her embrace to put my cheek against hers, as is their custom, I look at a picture - so old it has turned brown - it has a large inlaid frame made in Isfahan. The picture shows a young bride and her groom; neither of the two is over twenty years old. The bride is definitely Maggie; her big blue eyes, filled with an expression between bewilderment and curiosity, now smaller and not so curious, but completely bewildered, are still set in her wrinkled face. It is hard to believe that John was such a handsome and graceful man sometime in his youth. The picture bears no resemblance to the John whom I saw four days ago for the last time; it does not even resemble the John whom I saw ten years ago for the first time, with those worried and distressed eyes whose fear and anxiety could not be concealed even behind his eyeglasses.

He greeted me and all of a sudden said, "You should congratulate me today; it's my birthday." Like the English, I said, "Ah... Happy birthday!" I thought he could not be English; he had a slight accent which resembled the Irish.

"Guess how old I am." I looked at his gaunt face, gray hair and his teeth, which would wobble while he talked. He seemed over seventy to me; nevertheless, to make him happy, I said, "You can't be more than sixty years old." He laughed and said, "I'm sixty-four." I raised my eyebrows and, like the English, said, "Oh...No! I can't believe it." He looked around nervously and, while smiling triumphantly, said, "Yes, sixty-four. Today, I turned sixty-four."

Maggie invites me to sit down on one of the easy chairs across the room from John's corpse. There is a small old Baluchi rug spread on the floor under my feet; some of the flowers in the floral pattern of the rug are hidden under the box containing John's body.

Maggie continues to talk and speaks about the memories of the trip that they made to Spain a year ago. The person whom she is speaking to is a large woman with blonde hair; I have seen her in the street many times. I think it must be Elizabeth. Behind Elizabeth, on a brown cabinet full of chinaware, there are several picture frames, two of them inlaid wooden frames. One of them holds the picture of a young man who seems to be John when he was young; he is standing beside a tree and, behind him, there is the front gate of the monument *Chehel-sotun*. The other one holds the picture of the same young man, slightly younger, standing with an old man and an old woman who is wearing a chador, but does not veil her face. The old man resembles more the John whom I know than the young man in the picture. I think they must be John's parents, an Isfahani couple, and the young man is John when his name was still "Javad".

The other silver and gold-plated picture frames hold the pictures of people whom I have never seen; however, I think they must be John and Maggie's children and grandchildren. In one of the pictures, John is seen embracing a little girl who must be his granddaughter. This picture bears the most resemblance to the John I know, with that smile which was always on his face, as if a permanent feature, and with those ever-distressed and worried eyes.

I miss him so much. Although I have not seen him for only four days, I miss him. For almost ten years, I would see him most days in the morning every time I left home. He would start talking before I could open my mouth to greet him. He would talk about the people in the apartment next door to ours, which was three apartments down from his, and would say, "They've just moved into the neighborhood and nobody knows what kind of people they are." He would talk about the neighbor across the way, David, whose dog had been suffering from a disease that weakens the bones. And he would talk about Elizabeth, saying, "She's spending all of her time on propagandizing for the Conservative Party and does not understand what will happen to England if they are elected once again." He would talk about Michael with whom he used to work in the Communist Party and say, "These days, out of necessity, he has to work at the Grey Lion Hotel where the members of the National Front have their meetings every week." And he would talk about...

I do not know any of these people, but I know everything about them. perhaps I have seen some or all of them in the street, at the park, at the neighborhood newsstand, whose Indian owner told me about John's death four days ago, or in the hallways that connect our apartments. Perhaps I have even greeted them and said to them, "What a beautiful day today!" or "The weather's awful today!" But I do not know who Elizabeth is, or which one is Steve, or Michael.

I did not even know Maggie, John's wife, until three years ago. Nevertheless, I knew that she was German and the Nazis had burnt her Jewish father and had executed her alleged communist mother. More than three years ago, on a Sunday, I met her with John at the park. John introduced us to each other. He called her "my beloved wife" and me "my dear loving friend". Since then, I had been saying to her with a familiar smile, "What a beautiful day!" or "What a terrible day!" every time we saw each other. One night when I saw her at the train station, she even gave me the news about the birth of their fourth grandchild in Australia before I heard it from John. More importantly, the day after John's death, she sent me a note, saying, "You're the first among our friends who's notified of the death of my beloved husband. On Thursday, we'll accompany his body from home to the High Gate Cemetery."

Maggie is a loving and warm-blooded woman; John, however, was something else. He was kind and sincere even from the first days of our friendship; it was as if he had known me for a long time. But he never gave me a chance to talk; he never asked me a question, or when he did, my answer was limited to yes or no, or a sentence at the most. He would not let the answer be longer.

"Did you hear the news this morning?"

"What news?"

"The news about the bomb explosion at the Victoria Train Station!"

"Ah...Yes..." And, like the English, I would say, "Oh..God, what terrible news..."

Most of the days I wanted to talk, too. I wanted to ask him, "Did you hear the newsbrief on BBC 4? Did you hear that the Iraqis dropped eleven bombs on Isfahan, four bombs on Hamadan, and eighteen bombs on Tehran?" I wanted to tell him, "Forty-five people were executed in Iran today."

And most of the days I wanted to tell him, "I wish I could have been there when my father died," or "I miss my mother so much," or "Will it be possible to see my brother someday?" Or "Do you know my niece turned fourteen today? When I left, she was only three years old."

But I never got a chance. He never gave me the chance to talk. I know now that he deliberately did not let me talk, and I do not know why. He did not even ask me, "Where do you come from?" or "What's your nationality?" The first time he asked me my name, he repeated it without any accent and said, "What a beautiful name!" I was about to tell him what my name meant when he laughed and said, "Butterfly!" Surprised, I looked at him, but before I could ask him how he knew, he quickly changed the subject and went on about some new topic. At first I wondered if he talked about me with the other neighbors, what would he say? But, I realized that he would not talk to the other neighbors very much; he would listen most of the time. I saw him many times in the street or at the park, standing and listening to others very carefully. But with me he was the one who talked... and talked.

Every day when I left my apartment, he was there, outside, as if waiting for me. In those five or six minutes that he would walk with me to the train station—he said he was on his way to the park for his daily walk—it was only him who was talking, like a father who was telling a story to his daughter to amuse her. He would talk and tell his stories one after another—stories that were about everywhere and everyone except our common birthplace.

Our friendship was four years old when I found out the he was also Iranian. It was on the first day of the Iranian New Year when I saw him in the hallway and, like the English, I said, "You should congratulate me today." With a smile, he said, "Happy New Year!" Surprised, I asked, "How do you know that today's the beginning of our New Year?" Worried, he looked around and softly said, "I'm an Iranian, too." As usual he wanted to change the subject, but I could not resist anymore and asked him in Persian, "Why didn't you tell me, then?" "I don't know Persian." He said in English, "I don't remember anything about Iran at all. Anything!" Then, he quickly left as if he was afraid of something or someone. After that, I never talked about our birthplace. I wanted neither to annoy him nor to lose his companionship. Yet, there were many days when I had hoped not to see him—days when I did not feel like socializing and wanted to be alone. But, for the past four days, I had missed him every day.

The old man who, I guess, must be Michael, tells Maggie, "We should get going."

I think he has a slight accent; I cannot figure out where he is from, but he looks Greek. I size up his tall stature and broad shoulders; I cannot imagine him in the gaudy uniform of the doorman of the Grey Lion Hotel.

Maggie gets up; the men, who have come to bear away the corpse, are forming a ring around the box containing John's dead body. I am choked with sadness and tears are about to run down my face. I turn around to face the bookshelf behind me; like the

English, I do not want anyone to see my tears. On the top shelf, the oldest and the most worn-out book is titled, in Persian, *The Complete Poetical Works of Hatef of Isfahan.*[8] I take it off the shelf and open it. The margins of each page are filled up with notes and poems, written in a beautiful and legible script; these notes, all in Persian, are dated, some of them written this very year.

The coffin has been taken out and there is nobody left in the room.

---

[8] Hâtef (18th century) was among the early exponents of the neo-classical movement to restore the relative simplicity and elegance of the old masters. He is the author of a famous mystical Tarji`-band (Stanzaic poem), which has been translated by E.G. Browne.

14

Setareh in the Mist

Shokuh Mirzadegi

He closes the teach-yourself Swedish book and listens to the breathing of the man who has just entered Setareh's room: the long muffled howling of a dying dog resounds in the hollow of his head and turns to twisted images of mating dogs, which his playmates try to separate with sticks and stones. The dogs howl but do not separate; they wriggle against one another, in between life and death, baring their teeth, and the foam of their mouths is scattered in the air like white specks of powder. He, frightened and anxious, is glued to the wall; his fear of dogs prevents him from joining in the attack with his friends.

He puts aside the teach-yourself Swedish book. The man's breathing and the images of the dogs will not let him be. He begins walking about the room; he gazes at the windows, the panes of which have been broken for months. He looks at his children, at Cyrus, who has been asleep for a while, and at Senobar, the pupils of whose eyes are still visible beneath her drooping eyelashes like two big dark blue pearls, just like those in Setareh's eyes.

He takes off his glasses, rubs them with his fingers and takes a deep breath. His breathing merges with the sound of the man's breath and a hot sweaty rage rushes at him, like the monster which would rise at night from the midst of the ancient desert opposite his childhood house and grow bigger and bigger, turning round and round, forming a funnel through which it would climb up to the moon. The dust would pound on the window of the room where he slept. It had been two weeks since the man came. He would come and go. Whenever the man was not there, he would feel completely empty inside: with no trace either of pain or of serenity. But whenever the man came, he grew agitated and confused and did not know how to deal with it. He would be quiet - just grew more and more quiet. The greater his agitation and confusion, the more silent he became.

For months, he had not talked to anybody, except to say a few routine words. He would not even return Setareh's greetings any more. Except for two or three common phrases, he would not even talk to his kids. From early in the morning, when he went out to walk aimlessly in the streets, drink tea at the cafes and read his teach-yourself Swedish books in libraries, until evening, when he would anxiously and hesitantly return home, he did not speak a word to anyone. Whenever he arrived, Setareh would have just finished setting the table for dinner. He would sit at the table and eat in silence; he would not look at Setareh, who would be speaking with their four year-old twins. The kids only talked to Setareh, having apparently realized that they would get their answers only from their mother.

When dinner was over, he would take the kids to their room where they would play for an hour or two and then fall asleep; he would not talk to them very much. When they were playing or sleeping, he would sit on the chair upright and motionless and stare at the teach-yourself book which lay open on his lap.

He had become a scarecrow, making sure the kids did not run outside or beat each other about the head and shoulders. But he seemed to be concentrating on Setareh all the time. He knew all her movements and routines, which had gradually assumed a fixed schedule, without even looking at her.

He knew that when he was taking the kids to their room, Setareh would quickly wash the dishes and tidy up the kitchen. He knew when she would go upstairs, or when she would put on her violet or green dress—the two dresses that would reveal her neck, shoulders and half of her breasts. She wore them only at this time at night.

He knew when she would sit at her dressing table to put on green or dark blue eyeshadow, anoint her eyes with collyrium and paint a line from the corner of each eye to the bridge of her nose— a line that would make her languishing dark blue eyes more beautiful. And he knew when she would let her chestnut brown hair hang down on her neck and shoulders.

He stands behind the cracked window, which remains taped up even though the war is over, thinking about a thick curl of Setareh's hair which covers her left breast, the glowing skin revealed in her violet or green dress.

He was always focussed on Setareh, even as he answered his kids' childish questions. Hearing her footsteps on the stairs, he would know that it was time for the men to come. He knew that every night after preparing herself, Setareh would go and sit in the kitchen in the dark in order to be close to the courtyard door and open it as soon as the bell rang.

The first client would usually arrive around seven o'clock. After him, the bell would ring six more times. And every night he would count the seven times that the clients would go up and come down the stairs. Sometimes, like tonight, he could hear the client's lusty breathing, but he could never hear any sound from Setareh. So, where was she then? He knew that he would not see her until the next morning when she would feed the kids and caress them.

It wasn't like this until two months ago. He knew that after the last client left, Setareh would tidy up the room and open the windows. She would toss her green or violet dress on the bed and take a bath. He knew that it would take her half an hour to bathe, and that she would scrub her head and body hard, as if she wanted to peel a layer of skin off. Then, she would dry her hair and pin it up behind her head, as she wore it during the day. She would put on a dress, which was neither violet nor green, and would come downstairs to spread her mattress in the corner of the living room, which had become their bedroom for the past eight months, next to where she would spread his mattress.

The man's breathing interferes with the memories of those days.

Setareh would curse Heaven and Earth and those who had de-

stroyed everything and made her life so miserable. Most nights,
her words ended in soft choked-back sobs. He would go and sit
by Setareh's side; he would embrace her and caress her hair, and
Setareh would give herself up to his soothing. But neither of them
wanted to sleep in the same bed or make love. Setareh would not
even let him kiss her face; she would only lay her head upon his
lap and groan sadly, and he would comfort her while caressing her
hair, "It'll be over. It'll one day be over. We'll leave this desolate
place. We'll go to Sweden. Not too much longer!"

And Setareh would find comfort and fall asleep in her vague
dreams about Sweden...

But he had been unable to even talk to Setareh since that hot
sweaty rage overtook him. He had grown sullen and cross with
her, though they had not quarreled or fought. Setareh did not
complain about it either. Perhaps she believed he was right, or she
thought if she were him, she would be in the same mood as he.
Nevertheless, two months ago when he told Setareh that Baqerlu
had decided to send more clients to their house every night, she
suddenly began to complain and he, uncontrollable, threw her to
the corner of the room. Her head hit the wall. Setareh held her
head between two hands and said, "Why are you bullying me?
Why are you hitting me instead of hitting him?" And he shouted,
"Shut up, you whore!"

He sits by Cyrus's side and looks at his half-open mouth, which
looks like his own mouth when he was a kid - a kid who had once
opened his mouth to say, "Shut up, woman!" to his mother but was
unable to say it. The cat had devoured all of the fish in the pond
and was still sitting on the other side of the courtyard, licking its
paws. Its eyes looked like those of a tiger ready to attack. And
Cyrus had thrust the strainer into the water to pull the last fish out
of the pond. He wanted to throw that one to the cat as well to stop
the cat from looking at him.

"What are you doing? You, stupid clumsy boy! Why are you
catching the fish instead of kicking the cat out?"

He had gathered his mattress and taken it to the children's
room to sleep there every night after that. It was then that he had
felt sorry for Setareh.

Tonight when he looks at the dark blue pupils of Senobar's

eyes, which can be seen through her half-open eyelashes, he feels sorry for Setareh once again. He often pitied Setareh: those nights when they slept in the same room without saying a word to each other. For a long time, he would gaze at Setareh's decent face, which looked innocent and childlike under the dim light outside the window. He knew that she was suffering, too. That was why he pitied her. He wanted to tell her, "It'll be over. If we leave this desolate place, everything will be okay. Perhaps we can even forget these days." He wanted to say that, but he could not.

He could not even look at Setareh's face any more. For two months, he had not looked at her, not even once when they would sit for a few minutes at the table to have breakfast or dinner. He would see her though and would observe her movements and behavior. He would see the supple movement of her hands, the charming twist in her glimpse, the tilting of her neck and the beautiful quiver of her lips when she was talking to the kids and adoring them. Without looking at her, he would see that she was still as pretty as she was seven years ago when they met each other for the first time.

Something acrimonious and painful separates him from the past. The man's lusty breathing reaches its peak, and he shakes with anger; something as thick as hatred spins inside him — hatred of this sound, of this man, of all of the men whose shadows he could see grow larger and larger on the cracked glass of the courtyard window as they passed by. By the time they reached the building, their long shadows would pass the top of the tall plane tree in the middle of the coutyard. At this point, that gigantic monster would stir and, restored to life, come right up to the window. Sometimes when the spinning funnel picked up speed, it would hoist the dust and pebbles on the ground up into the air and drive them against the window pane. Once the window even broke and the dust and dirt poured in—so much dirt that it could cover his small body and bury him alive.

"I hate this one most of all." He could recognize this one by his muffled moaning and his heavy breathing.

Every morning after this client had spent time with Setareh, he would feel that the young men in the neighborhood would give him a different look, which he knew very well. It was like the look he would give to Nosrat's brother whenever Nosrat wore a mini-skirt and looked straight into the eyes of the boys she was talking to and smiled. Perhaps the client's voice could be heard by the neighbors, just as it would carry to the lower level. These very noises would make him infamous.

Many times he had thought that perhaps if Setareh were not so pretty, nobody would have suspected anything. Perhaps if she were not so pretty, Baqerlu would have helped them out, without making such a proposal . Perhaps...

As the man's breathing turns to shallow gasps, he remembers that Setareh, in that same argument that they had two months ago, had told him, "Did I ask this to happen? Wasn't it you who made the suggestion?"

He remembers that these words had driven him crazy and had made him pound on Setareh's chest with his fist. But, he still does not remember how he had told Setareh about Baqerlu's proposal. He does not remember at all how this happened or how they agreed to such a proposal. He realizes that his memory is fading and he does not know why. He cannot recognize the voice he hears in his head, which would cross out and delete everything from his memory. But Senobar's face, feverish due to diphtheria, is before his eyes. This was the time when they were absolutely penniless. He also remembers the letter bearing the order to expel him from his job because he was guilty of having two letters of recommendation from the former regime. It had been almost a year since the date of that letter. Senobar's throat was so infected she couldn't breathe. There was nobody else to borrow from. In extreme destitution, Baqerlu had suggested a solution. He remembers that his face had become hot like Senobar's face; the heat of his eyes steamed up his glasses. Out on the street, he wished he could find the strength to go back and kill Baqerlu. He does not remember why he did not do exactly that after hearing such a thing. He only remembers that at that moment Senobar's fever had gradually sapped and destroyed his courage, the way it would sap and destroy his flesh and blood.

He also remembers Setareh's eyes; immersed in tears, they had gazed at him. Setareh had cried quietly and said, "You'll be watching the kids from tomorrow on. I'll get work as a maid. After all, in such a big city with all these rich people, there must be a need for maids or cleaning ladies."

But there were no jobs available; diphtheria was choking the breath out of Senobar and Setareh, in tears, kept giving her sitz baths.

He remembers that he sat stupefied looking at mother and daughter until Setareh finally looked at him and said, "If there's no God, one must seek help from Satan. Get up and call Baqerlu."

And Baqerlu had said, "Wise decision! Don't even worry about it. I'll only send respectable clients and I myself will get the money from them. At the end of each week, I'll bring the money so that there will be no problem. I'll also ask the neighborhood *Komiteh* to keep watch all around your house."

Every Thursday, the last client was Baqerlu himself. Half of most of the money was deposited in a safe on which he had glued the very first postcard his sister had sent them from Sweden. He remembers that the safe has been sitting in the living room in their wardrobe since he moved to that room eight months ago. He goes and opens the wardrobe. Stockholm smiles at him with its snow-covered lakes and its buildings, short and tall. The smile brings out gooseflesh all over his body. He hears the man's footsteps on the stairs. He looks at his watch; it is a few minutes past ten. Evidently, their business is over sooner than on previous nights. He returns to the kids' room and looks at the children for a long time. When he hears the slamming of the courtyard gate, he feels that something has lit up in his mind, but the voice he hears in his head has deleted everything from his memory.

He softly goes to the kitchen, opens the drawer and grabs something; he cannot tell what he has picked up. On the wall calendar beside the door, he sees the slopes of the Alborz Mountains in summer. For a moment, he stops and looks at the corn-roses which have turned to small black spots in the dark. The voice in his head orders him to move. He turns and goes upstairs. It appears to him that tonight he can climb up these stairs very comfortably, smoothly and naturally, as he could each night a few months ago.

When he reaches the bedroom door, he stops for a moment. He can see without looking inside; Setareh is tidying up the bed, she has not opened the windows yet. He opens the door and sees Setareh still lying on their wedding bed, naked and still, like a plaster statue which has just been taken out of its mould. Her hair, however, is lively and shiny; it is spread on the pillow and around her pale face. Setareh is clutching the edge of her green dress with one hand, as though it were a flag. O God! She is so beautiful.

The plaster statue moves as soon as she sees him and quickly covers her breast and belly with the green dress. She wants to get up but, frightened and unbelieving, remains in her place.

He calmly approaches Setareh. The feverish steam blurs his glasses for a moment and Setareh disappears behind the mist. But he does not stop moving towards her; he comes next to her, sleeping in the mist, and suddenly and quickly thrusts the knife in between her milkwhite breasts. The sound of her bones breaking mingles with the long sigh coming out of her half-open mouth. He wants to pull the knife out, but he cannot. The long blade has got caught in the bones around her heart. He takes off his glasses and wipes his eyes with the back of his hand. He sees Setareh is looking at him from afar, very far, with wide-open eyes, with neither astonishment nor fear.

Whenever he would come to their bedroom, Setareh would be lying in their bed. As soon as she saw him, she would raise her left hand and beckon him to come to her. He takes Setareh's left hand and lifts it up; he finds no invitation in it. Filled with horror, he steps back; Setareh's hand falls and her eyes gently close.

He puts his glasses on. Behind the mist, he sees a smile shining on Setareh's lips—the smile which, in the past, long ago, would always bloom on her face after every love-making. His mind at peace, he turns and looks around. Out in the desert behind the cracked windows, the wind is still and the moon is rising.

Farkhondeh Aqâee was born in 1956 in Tehran. She went to school there, and obtained a Master's degree in sociology from the University of Tehran. Her career as a writer began with the publication of stories in a traditional realist style, but she has developed an interest in various experimental forms and techniques of writing. In 1987 she published a collection of allegorical short stories, entitled *The Green Hills* (*Tapeh-hâ-ye sabz*). Her most recent collection of short stories, *The Little Secret* (*Râz-e kuchek*), was published in 1993 and won the prestigious Gardun Literary Prize in Iran. She currently lives in Tehran with her husband and their two children, a twelve year-old daughter and nine year-old son.

The story *"The First Day of the New Year's Festival"* (*"Ruz-e avval-e 'ayd"*), in the collection *Râz-e kuchek* (Tehran: Sherkat-e Châp-e Khvâjeh, Fall 1993, pp. 81-90) treats the religious, spiritual and practical sides of a death in the family, the mother-daughter relationship, and the sense of helplessness that the traditional dependence of women on men in Iranian culture can create.

15

The First Day of
the New Year's Festival
Farkhondeh Aqaee

T he last night of the winter was almost over and the morning would bring with it the first day of spring and the New Year's festival.[9] Esmat finished her dinner and washed her plate and teacup. She took a package of meat out of the freezer, put it on the lower shelf in the refrigerator to thaw for tomorrow and came back into the room. For half an hour now, her mother had not made a sound. From sunset until supper time she had been wheezing, as she did every night, and now she was resting peacefully. Esmat looked at the clock. It was past eleven. She checked her mother's medicine bottles and carefully poured some medicine out of a half-empty bottle into a spoon. She slipped one of her hands under her mother's head to raise it, and with the other hand held the spoon ready to pour the medicine down her throat. But her mother wouldn't open her mouth. Esmat called her. There

---

[9] The Persian New Year starts on March 21, the spring equinox. The first month of the Persian calendar begins on this day, corresponding to the astrological sign of Aries. The Naw Ruz, or New Year's festivities, continue for twelve days in Iran.

was no response. Alarmed, Esmat shook her and laid her head on her mother's chest. Her heart had stopped.

Esmat pounded on her chest with her fists: "O God! In the name of Muhammad, the Prophet, why is this tragedy happening to me?!"

The doctors had lost all hope for her mother months ago. They had said her illness was old age and she would remain alive till she stopped breathing. She thought of her sister who was now in Isfahan, and her brother who had gone on a trip to the North with his family just yesterday.

Esmat thought, "I vow to perform fifty prayers; just let my brother call." Everyone had lost hope in her mother's recovery some time ago, even though her death still seemed improbable. Everyone had grown accustomed to having her around: sick, in pain and moaning, and with each breath she drew, you thought it would be her last, but she had kept at it for months. Esmat would sit beside her and take her in her arms like a child. She would give her her food. She would take her to the bath and wash her. Now she was dead and the nightmare of her mother's death, which had troubled her sleep for years and years, had come to pass, at eleven p.m. on the last night of the year.

Esmat pulled the sheet over mother's face. She put on her chador and went into the hallway. The neighbors' lights were all out and the hallway was plunged in silence and darkness. She went downstairs. She knew Maryam Khanoom better than the other neighbors. Esmat stood at the door of her apartment and gently tapped on it a few times with her fingertip. No one answered. She was fearful of disturbing the quiet of the hallway and did not want to ring the bell at that time of the night. She hurried back upstairs, closed the door and shut herself up in her room. She was afraid to go look at her mother. She couldn't think what to do. She picked up the receiver, but didn't know anyone in town she could call. She would not have been so helpless if her sister were there or if her brother had not gone out of town. She should have let Maryam Khanoom know. Maryam Khanoom was a sensible woman, she would definitely be a big help. She found Maryam Khanoom's number in the phone book and called. Still half asleep, Maryam Khanoom's teenage son answered the phone.

Esmat hurriedly introduced herself and apologized. She asked to speak with the boy's mother.

"Mom went to Qazvin to see Auntie this morning. She'll be back tomorrow or the day after."

It now occurred to Esmat that perhaps the boy could do something about it.

"Sorry to call at this time of night, but my mother...My mother has passed away. I thought that, maybe, if Maryam Khanoom had been home..."

The boy shouted, "Your mother has passed away? May God bless her soul! My condolences." And his voice began trembling. "Have you notified Emergency? Would you like me to call them?"

"I hadn't thought of it. I'll call immediately. If only I wasn't alone. If only Maryam Khanoom were here."

"I'll go to Qazvin tomorrow morning. I'll let my mother know."

"It won't make any difference tomorrow. In fact, don't mention it to her. Sorry to bother you at this time of night. Good Bye!"

She was greatly embarrassed about having given the boy a fright. She disconnected the line and quickly called Emergency.

"Hello, Emergency? Excuse me, my mother has passed away."

"You have to notify *Behesht-e Zahra* Cemetery."

"I thought perhaps you could help."

"Is she still breathing?"

She could not lie. "No, she has been ill for a few months, but it's been an hour since she stopped breathing."

"Then, we can't do anything for you. You have to contact the *Behesht-e Zahra* Cemetery."

She called the Cemetery.

"Ma'am, at this time of the night, we have no one on duty. Call again in the morning. And you must have a death certificate."

"The doctors know all about it. My mother had been ill for a long time."

"Nothing doing without the Certificate of Death. You must have the birth certificate, too."

"Well, what can I do right now? Alone with my mother! We don't have anybody here."

"Are you afraid all alone?"

Esmat suddenly came to her senses. "Afraid? Of what? She

was talking to me up to an hour ago. Who's afraid of their own mother?"

After that she called the doctor. There was no answer, as if someone had pulled the phone plug.

After months of being confined to bed, mother's death was not unexpected, but, coming at this particular hour, Esmat had panicked. Overwhelmed, she went back to the room, pulled the sheet back off her mother's face and sat down beside her. Mother's face was calm and yellowish. Esmat embraced her and tightly pressed her to her chest. She touched her mother's forehead; it was cold. She spread out some blankets. She thought she had better not turn out the light. She lay down beside her mother. She took her mother's hands and held them. She closed her eyes, but could not sleep. She was numb. At any moment she expected her mother to call out to her:

"Esmat, are you asleep? What about my medicine? Isn't it past time for the next dosage?"

"Esmat, are you asleep? Get up and open the window. I'm hot."

"Esmat, are you asleep? I think you forgot to lock the door. Get up and check."

She got up and looked at her mother. Mother was asleep. She wasn't talking; her lips were not moving. It was the first night her mother slept peacefully, without rousing Esmat every minute. She used to say that she could not sleep and that she was waiting for death. She's afraid of going to bed and dying in her sleep. Now Esmat thought about sitting up and reading the Koran until morning came, but she didn't feel like it. She didn't want to read the Koran for her until her corpse was in the grave. She took one of mother's books off the shelf above her head. She had been reading for her mother for a long time. Ever since they brought her home from the hospital. She opened the scarlet cover of the book. The words were large and legible. She opened the book to a page which had been marked by a thick string. She read aloud:

"Praise upon thee, my lord and son of my lord. Thou seest
my station and hearest my words and returneth my greetings, and thou livest near thy Lord and art nourished. In

truth, the sins which keep me back from God have weighed down upon my back and keep me from my sleep. Memory of them disturbs my inner being, and I have fled toward God, the Mighty and Majestic. Be, therefore, an intercessor for me before God, and a refuge from the Fire, my supporter during my days, and my guide on the Bridge of Sirât, and my companion and friend in the grave...."[10]

She felt her eyelids getting heavy. Her head slumped over the open page of the book. Someone was calling her, "Esmat, are you asleep? Get up and give me a drop of water."

She woke up with a start. Was it mother calling her? She looked at her; she was lying cold and quiet. She felt that her mother's throat was moving and ran to the kitchen. She brought a glass of water, opened her mother's mouth and, with a small spoon, poured a bit of water down her throat. Her mother drank the first and second spoonfuls, then her teeth clenched and the water trickled out. Esmat could see the path which the water was taking down her mother's throat. She wiped her mother's lips with a napkin. Alas, if her mother died thirsty, how could she tell her sister and brother? "O God! I vow to say a hundred prayers if my brother calls before morning."

She picked up the book and read aloud for mother:

> "O thou who art friend to the friendless; O thou who art physician to him who hath no physician; O thou who answereth the prayers of him who hath none to listen to him; O thou who art kind to him who hath no comforter. O guide, O confidant, O companion, O protector, O concealer of sins, O all-powerful, O patient one, O beloved, O conqueror, O friend! O leader, O master, O most merciful of the merciful; O most revered goal and kindest of all those

---

[10] This would appear to be a prayer to Husayn, son of `Ali, and grandson of the prophet, the fourth Imam of the Shiites, who was martyred on the plain of Karbala in 680. He and `Ali are the major focal points of Shiite devotional piety and worship. In Muslim eschatology, The Bridge of Sirât must be crossed to enter heaven. It is as thin as a sword and those whose deeds are unholy tumble off into hell.

who are besought. I have come towards thee seeking thy
nearness. Make me not hopeless in my endeavor and cut
me not off from hope, by thy grace. Ordain for me honor in
this world and the next, near unto thee, and make me one of
those who are nigh unto thy court, O most merciful of the
merciful.....

Her eyes closed and her head felt heavy. She dreamt that she was
with her brother and her father and her husband. It was the last
time that she had seen her husband. They were arguing. They
were standing on either side of her, yelling at each other—the
same old things:

"Why don't you find a job?" — "Don't interfere in our lives." —
"You good-for-nothing!" — "Did you think she had nobody?" —
"Do you beat her up, too?"—"Are you going to go on renting forever?"— "I can make a living anywhere." — "Did you think she
had no family to support her?" — "I've heard you're an addict..."

They had surrounded her, dragging her this way and that. The
very next day her husband left for good. First, they said he may
have died; then they said he had been seen in Shiraz. Later on,
they received word that he was working in an inn in Zahedan.
Years later, someone said that they had seen him and that he was
doing very well for himself. He had married and had a few children.

Esmat was still dizzy in her sleep and kept hearing her mother
calling her:

"Esmat, Esmat! Are you asleep again? It's past time for my
medicine. Get up! Are you asleep again? Dead asleep?"

She woke up startled. It was her mother calling her again. She
sensed that her mother's eyes had been open, and that she had
closed them as soon as Esmat woke up. She seemed silent and
cold. She thought, what if her brother doesn't call tomorrow?
What if he doesn't bring mother's birth certificate? What if she
can't find the doctor. Mother's corpse would have to stay there for
several days. With no burial certificate, no guardian, no father, no
husband, and no brother? The thought crossed her mind: "I vow
to say two hundred prayers if my brother calls by morning, by six
a.m."

She looked at the clock; it was still one a.m. She flipped

through the pages of the book and read for mother:

> "O thou innocent one, O oppressed one, O thou afflicted by
> tribulations, O guiding master! O pure flesh! May God slay
> those who have slain thee and damn those who have tyr-
> annized thee with their hands and their words. O my lord
> and intercessor! I swear by thee and thy forebearers, and
> thy pure, innocent followers. O heir to Adam; chosen of
> God; heir to Noah; heir to Abraham, the friend of God; heir
> to Moses, who spoke with God; heir to Jesus, the spirit of
> God; heir to Muhammad; O thou, the friend of God! Thou
> art the blood desired by God and the son of the blood de-
> sired by God, the blood that is sought out and searched for.
> Thou didst obey God until death overtook thee. May God
> curse that people which oppressed thee and that people
> who heard the news and were content with it. I bear wit-
> ness that thou wert a brilliant light in the loins of thy noble
> forefathers and in the wombs of thy pure foremothers..."

Her head drooped on the book and sleep filled her eyes. Someone
was calling her from afar. Louder and louder, someone was
shouting: "Esmat, Esmat, are you asleep? It's cold. Did you close
the window? It's getting colder, too cold."

It was mother calling her. Startled, she opened her eyes. She
looked at the clock. It was almost dawn. What if her brother
wouldn't come, if he wouldn't call... She vowed to say three hundred prayers if her brother would come soon. She could hear the
call to dawn prayer in the distance. If she could have, if she didn't
first have to perform the ritual ablutions after touching the dead, if
her legs could have held her up, and if her heart weren't beating so
fast, she would have said her morning prayer. She took the sheet
off her mother's body, straightened it out and carefully spread it
again over her body, smoothing it out. She went to the closet and
opened her mother's suitcase. Years ago, her mother had put that
suitcase away. She took her mother's robe out of the suitcase and
laid it down by her head. The suitcase was full of yellowed sugar
cones, the dust of the holy threshold[11], a few packs of dried ciga-

---

[11] Probably from the shrine of 'Ali or Husayn in Iraq, centers of Shiite pilgrimage. Iranians often take sugar cubes on pilgrimage, lay them on the

rettes, which had been put aside for the days of mourning, and a
hand-woven cashmere shroud to cover the coffin. Her mother had
thought of everything. Esmat returned the suitcase to the closet
and went back to her mother. She opened the book and read it to
her:

> "O God! May I enter? O Messenger of God! May I enter?
> O Commander of the Faithful! May I enter? O my Lady,
> Fatimeh, the resplendent, the best of all women on earth!
> May I enter? O my lord, Hasan ebn Ali, Husayn ebn Ali,
> Ali ebn Husayn ebn Zayn al-Abedin, Muhammad ebn Ali,
> Jafar ebn Muhammad, Musa ebn Jafar, Ali ebn Musa al-
> Reza, Muhammad ebn Ali, Ali ebn Muhammad, Hasan ebn
> Ali! O Lord of the Age![12] May I enter? O guardian angels
> who reside in and surround this shrine! May I enter?..."[13]

Esmat choked with tears and wept bitterly. She felt her mother's
hand on her shoulder: "Esmat, Esmat, why are you crying?"
  She looked at her mother, at her ever-sad eyes, which would
cause every question to freeze on her lips. She read:

> "To Him will I return, and from Him I will ask that he ac-
> cept the repentance of this lowly, humble, fearful, needy,
> helpless and tearful servant, him who hath no control over

---

holy thresholds to bless them and eat them medicinally in case of severe
illness.

[12] These are the names of the Imams in Twelver Shiism. The Twelfth
Imam, who is believed by Shiites to be in occultation, is known as the
Lord of the Age, and when he returns, he will rid the world of injustice.
The messenger of God refers to Muhammad, and Ali, his designated
successor, is known as the Commander of the Faithful. Fatimeh is the
daughter of Muhammad and wife of Ali, the mother of the line of Imams.
The Imams are appealed to as intercessors with God, begging remission
of sins for the Shiite faithful.

[13] This is a prayer said by Shiites when making pilgrimage to the shrines
of Ali and Husayn.

his profit, his loss, his death and his life, nor his resurrection..."

It was long past six o'clock. She thought she would not even say one prayer. O God! All these prayers! What if my brother doesn't come, what if he doesn't call, what should I do? Tired and distressed, she got up and went to the window. It was the first day of the New Year's Festival, but the streets still seemed to be deserted. A chilling draft was coming through the crevice of the window pane.

> "May my father and mother be a sacrifice for you! The land in which ye are buried and achieved your desires is clean and pure. O ye, who have succeeded in obtaining your desires, would that I were there with you to achieve my desires..."

She went towards her mother. Her mother's face had been filled with the morning light. She was as cold as ice. Esmat embraced her and pressed her to her chest - that small yellow wilted body! Many times she had read this passage to her:

> "My heart hath mingled with your heart and my affairs depend upon yours. May God's mercy be upon you and upon your bodies and your frames, and upon your presence and your absence, and upon that which is manifest and hidden in you. Benedictions upon you, O oppressed ones, O sons of the oppressed..."

She became aware of the constant ringing of the phone. She left her mother and ran to her room. O God! Fifty, a hundred, a thousand prayers.....

She picked up the phone, but her voice wouldn't obey her. Her throat was dry. On the other end was her brother, who kept asking, "Esmat? Esmat? Is that you?"

With a trembling voice, she answered: "Brother, where have you been?"

"I can barely hear you. Last night, I kept having nightmares. How is mother?"

The woman hesitated for a moment. She put all her energy into her voice. "They wouldn't take her anywhere. They wouldn't take her anywhere. She wasn't accepted anywhere. Get her birth certificate and bring it."

The receiver slipped from her unresponsive hands. Her face was red-hot. She choked back her tears and went to the window. No longer fearful of mother, she opened the window so that the light and warmth of the first day of the New Year filled the entire room.

Summer, 1988

Mahkâmeh Rahimzâdeh was born in Iran. She has recently begun writing short stories, which have been published in Persian periodicals inside Iran. She contributes to the prestigious Persian literary journal *Gardun*, which has recently been closed by the Iranian authorities. Ms. Rahimzâdeh lives in Karaj, near Tehran.

Her story, *"The Pink Room"* (*"Otâq-e surati," Gardun*, no. 42 Tehran, 1993, pp. 50-52), told in flash-back style, depicts a college student's life abroad and her nostalgic longing to return to a childhood home that has been gradually but irretrievably slipping away in her absence.

16

The Pink Room
Mahkameh Rahimzadeh

Sahar hung up the phone and gazed at the bedside clock: twelve-thirty, that would make it eleven thirty in the morning, their time. She had talked for one hour and fifteen minutes. The phone bill this month would reach the sky. If she worked a few night shifts, she would be able to save enough to pay it. The pay at night was twice as much as the day rate, but she would get more tired and be less safe. As soon as a suspicious-looking person or a drunk would enter the store, she would run towards Mr. Harrison's room to wake him up. He had told her to do so himself. He used to sleep in a room at the far end of the store.

Sahar wrote, "Dear Simin, a bottle of sauce fell out of the hand of one the guys. Mr. Harrison shouted at him, 'I'm going to dock double its price from your paycheck—first, for the price of the bottle and second, for your carelessness.' He always acts like that. Even though he has a bad temper, I'd rather work for him than Mr. Douglas, who gives the weekly paycheck late, or Miguel, who would take liberties. By the way, don't tell Mom and Dad about Miguel."

Dad said, "Where do you work, sweetie? Is it a safe place or not?"

Sahar said, "Don't worry, Dad. I've got a good boss. The same man standing behind me in the picture; you saw what an old man he is. He likes people from the East. He calls me and Salimeh 'darling.'"

She had said the same thing to her father even when she was working in that Spanish restaurant, where Miguel would insist on driving her home every night, and every now and then she would feel unsafe.

Dad had bent to change the place of the big Cycas tree in the greenhouse. He said, "Don't keep bending her ear about going to America. I won't send my daughter abroad."

Mom was sitting facing the sun, plucking her eyebrows with a pair of tweezers. She said, "I wrote to my cousins about it. They said, 'Send her. We'll make the arrangements for her to go to college.'" The flowerpot slipped out of dad's hands. In a loud voice, he said, "Going abroad is expensive." Mom, indifferent, said, "She'll work. Haven't others worked?"

Sahar lay down on the bed. The light from the courtyard was shining into the room through the cracks of the Venetian blinds. No sound but the chirping of the crickets could be heard. She put one leg on the top of the other one; if she lay down on the bed with her body stretched out, the crown of her head would touch the headboard and her heels would touch the footboard. Most nights she slept diagonally. They had brought the bed up from the courtyard, she and Salimeh.

Salimeh said, "Wait. Perhaps you'll find one on sale."

She said, "Forget about it! There's only one more year to go."

Sahar asked, "Simin, where are Mom and Dad?" I've been calling home for a whole week solid and no one answers. I took the test in my Management course; it was the last one. I miss all of you awfully. I can't wait to receive my transcript. Salimeh will mail it to me. I've even bought the plane ticket. Simin, can you hear me?"

She wrote, "Simin, you can't imagine how much I miss our house, my tiny little room, the yard. I had the picture you sent me enlarged, the one you took in the corner of the courtyard beside the decorative palm tree. You know, there is a small park across from the apartment which Salimeh and I have rented. There are short box trees planted in one corner of the park with a bench between them. Whenever I get the chance, I go there and sit on the bench. I close my eyes and touch the wet surface of the box trees and I can see the courtyard of our house before my eyes. Do you remember those days when we used to pluck the cherry blossoms, where Dad could not see us, and shower each other with them, pretending that we were brides? The night when you got married, I was ringing up people's purchases in the store. With head hanging down, I pressed the buttons with one hand and wiped away the tears with the other. Mother, always with a jealous eye out for what the neighbors were doing, kindled the fire of desire to come here in my heart. For this, I won't forgive her."

Sahar could hear music. It was the black lady who lived upstairs. Whenever she couldn't sleep, she would take her boombox and go sit in the park. She would sit on the bench and listen to music. She was tall and strong and looked about sixty years old.

Whenever she drew one leg up and rested the sole of her foot on the bench, her knee would nearly reach her ears. She was living by herself. Every time she said, "My kids only send me a card on Mother's Day," tears would well up in her eyes. The black singer was singing one of the current popular American songs. In it he told his fellow countryman: "I know not when nor how you set foot on this land, but I know that both of us are lonely, both of us are strangers."

Sahar rolled over. Her gaze fell on the black stain on the carpet. They had bought the carpet from a Lebanese guy for three bucks. Sahar asked him, "Will you go back home?" The guy just stood there in silence, fixing his sad gaze on her. Salimeh had said, "I don't think there's any hope we'll ever go." Salimeh's eyes looked like Simin's - big and black. Her look always comforted Sahar.

Sahar said, "Simin, can you hear me? I'm coming home. I was going to tell Mom and Dad, but nobody answers their phone. Have they gone somewhere? They would never leave the house unattended. Simin, why don't you say something? Is there anything wrong?"

Having seen the plane ticket in Sahar's purse, Salimeh asked, "You're leaving for sure, then?" Salimeh held the mirror in front of her face so that Sahar wouldn't see her. She took out the black eyeliner and began making up her eyes. She sniveled; Sahar went to her and wiped the black smudges around Salimeh's eyes away with a paper tissue. She said, "Salimeh, I would never leave you alone here. As soon as I get there, I'll send you an invitation. There you'll be closer to Lebanon. Maybe it will even be possible for you to go to your relatives for a visit. We'll live together in my parent's house; you'll sleep in Simin's room. We have a big court-yard—my dad loves gardening. Exactly the opposite of my mother, who would like to live in a condominium."

The music stopped. Sahar put her finger between two slats of the Venetian blind and pressed down. The black lady wasn't there. She let go of the blinds and rubbed her finger against her jeans. She paced the length of the room and counted, "one, two, three, four..." She stopped, facing the wall. The room was eight paces long, smaller than Simin's room.

She had protested. Dad had said, "...because you're younger." Sahar had said, "Then, the color of the walls should be pink." Dad had agreed. Sahar used to call her room "dinky pink."

With thumbtacks she put posters on the walls - posters of the singers and actors she liked. One of the posters showed the land-scape of a rice paddy; this poster was a large one, as tall as Sahar. She had placed her bed by the window. Whenever she lay on the bed, she could see the entire yard. In the winter, she would talk to her snowmen from up there—the snowmen that she and Simin had made. In the spring and summer, as soon as she had opened her eyes she would greet the crimson roses growing in the flower-bed nearest her window. The sight of autumn always made her sad. She would look at the leaves hanging on the cherry tree, in various shades of yellow to brown. She would tell the trees, "Don't worry. Time flies. In the twinkle of an eye, the spring will come and you'll turn green."

The day she was coming to America, she stood in every corner of the room, and Simin took her picture from different angles.

At uncle's wedding, Mom and Dad had danced. Simin poked Sahar in the side with her elbow and said, "Look at the dog and cat!"

Dad's voice could be heard from behind the closed door: "Do you want to wear this? With that belt? I'm not going to come with you looking like that." Mom said, "You don't want to come, don't come. You should be proud to come with me."

Dad said, "You'll look like a clown."

Mom said, "Country bumpkin. You've got no taste."

Dad said, "You're right. If I had good taste, I wouldn't have married you."

Mom said. "It was my fault. I was deceived by your appearance. Why did I have to marry a shabby, destitute clerk?" She began to cry.

Sahar threw her chemistry book aside: "Ahh, damn them! They don't let me study."

Simin was moving and tossing about in bed. She said, "May you rot in hell!"

Both Mom and Dad cried at the airport. Mom wiped the tears off her face with a tissue; Dad just kept blinking rapidly and tightly closing his eyes. Simin and her fiance were waving.

Sahar squeezed her temples; she had a headache. She got up and took a pain-killer out of the medicine cabinet. She took out a beer can from the refrigerator and pulled the pop-top. The gas escaped with a muffled noise. She put the pill on her tongue and drank up the beer. The unwashed dishes were in the sink. Whenever Salimeh was impatient, she wouldn't do anything. During the past week, since she found out that Sahar was going to leave, she had been snapping at everyone like a mean dog. She wouldn't look in Sahar's eyes and when she went in her room, she would lock her door. When it was her turn, she wouldn't do the dishes or sweep the floor. Sahar went back to her own room, took out a lighter and a pack of cigarettes from her purse, lit a cigarette and lay on the bed. She laid the ashtray on her stomach.

"Dad, don't look so worried about me. I promise to do nothing but study."

"Miguel, please! How many times do I have to tell you that I won't come to your apartment?"

"Miguel, please stop the car. I want to go; I have a test tomorrow."

"Miguel, don't touch me."

Miguel said angrily, "You shouldn't work here any more."

She had been out of work for six months; she borrowed from a few friends to pay her tuition. At that time, she was living in the dorm.

Dad said, "Sahar, dear, I managed to scrape together a thousand dollars to send you. If you are really hard-up for money, I'll mortgage the house."

"Dad, don't even mention it, or I'll get upset. I'm not hard-up for money at all. I'm supposed to start work in this store soon; it pays three dollars an hour."

Mom wrote: "Dear Sahar, you look so thin in the picture. My friends saw the picture and couldn't believe that you were the same pretty Sahar they had seen in Iran. I told them that my kid was studying too hard. If you have a better picture, send it to me. I kiss you from afar. Love, Mom."

"What were you doing, Dad?"

"I'm painting the house."

"My room, too?"

"Yes, its turn will come."

"For God's sake, Dad, be careful of my posters. I'll come back in one hundred ninety-eight days. By the way, keep it the exact same shade of pink, Okay?"

"Pink it is!"

"Where's Mom?"

"Mom is getting ready for a party. Let me tell her to come talk to you."

"You see, Sahar? He always keeps himself busy with something or other to avoid coming to parties with me. I always have to go alone."

Sahar took deep puffs of the cigarette; the red circle around the white cylinder of the cigarette was beautiful. A cold breeze blew in through the half-open window. Sahar took a deep breath.

Mom said, "You must register the house half in my name."

Dad tossed the newspaper aside, "Why? Because your father helped me out?"

"My father wasn't obligated to help you. You must do as I say."

"Not a chance!"

Mom was sitting by the space heater, knitting. She threw the half-finished needlework aside, buried her face in her hands and wept bitterly.

Simin and Sahar said, "Dad, please! What difference does it

make? Mom is getting on our nerves with her crying."

Mom returned from the office of the notary public with a box of sweets; she kissed Simin and Sahar. Dad wasn't upset, either. He said jokingly, "Girls, watch your mother carefully. Remember not to do whatever she does."

Mom threw some orange peels at him and he snatched them in the air. Simin and Sahar laughed from the bottom of their hearts.

"Simin, dear, can you hear me? Where's Mom?"

"At Auntie's house."

"How long is she going to stay there?"

"I don't know... perhaps until she buys an apartment."

"What about Dad?"

"He sleeps in his office."

"I wish they would wait until I came back."

Sahar put out the cigarette with her thumb and laid the ashtray on the nighttable. It was five o'clock, which was four-thirty in the afternoon, their time.

"Simin, why did Dad give up?"

"Sahar, dear, your phone bill is running up."

"What the hell do I care! Tell me."

"Mom swallowed pills."

There was silence. Sahar asked, "Who bought it?"

"Sahar, dear, I can't hear you."

"I said, 'Who bought the house?'"

"A developer! He's demolished it; he wants to build an apartment complex."

Sahar took a deep breath. She asked, "How did Dad agree to live in an apartment?"

"He hasn't agreed."

"Then what's he going to do?"

The hair on Sahar's body stood on end. Her head was pounding. Her eyes were burning. The reddish-brown light crept in through the Venetian blinds. She closed her eyes. She drew a few deep breaths. Her stomach was upset. She had done the right thing not to tell Mr. Harrison about her plan to go back to Iran. She could keep her job. Salimeh would be so happy.

"Salimeh, how many years had you been living here when your house was bombed?"

"Don't ask me about it. I don't want to remember the past."

The door of the apartment opened and slammed shut. Sahar got up and wobbled into the hallway. Salimeh was sliding the chain into the slot on the door. She asked, "Are you still awake?"

Sahar took a few steps forward. She gazed into the dark pupils of Salimeh's eyes for a second, then hugged her and burst into tears.

Mehri Yalfâni was born in Hamadan. She received a degree in Electrical Engineering from the University of Tehran, and worked for nearly twenty years for the Ministry of Energy, the Water and Power Company of Khuzestan and the Electrical Company of Tehran. She began writing short stories while still in high school, and her first collection, *Happy Days* (*Ruz-hâ-ye khosh*) was published in 1966. She has also published two novels, *Before Autumn Comes* (*Qabl az pâ'iz*, 1980) and *Someone is Coming* (*Kasi mi-Âyad*, published in Sweden by Nashr-e Bârân, 1994). *Someone is Coming*, which tells about the life of a family in Hamadan during the nationalization of the Iranian Oil Company in the early 1950s, takes its title from a poem by the poetess Forugh Farrokhzâd, which fact, along with the vivid portrayals of the female characters in Yalfâni's stories, shows the growing influence of the previous generation of women writers on the current generation.

Yalfâni left Iran some time after the Revolution and has published a number of short stories in various Persian-language journals in the United States, such as *Forugh* and *Simorgh*, as well as a book-length collection called *The Birthday Party* (*Jashn-e tavallod*, Par Books, 1991). She has a new book in English, *Parastoo*, published by Women's Press [1995].

The title of her story *"Ringing the Bell With One Foot in the Grave"* (*"Zanguleh-ye pâ-ye tâbut,"* in *Simorgh*, 60 [Fall 1995], Mission Viejo, California, pp. 32-34) comes from a Persian idiom used when a man fathers a child at an advanced age. The story portrays two sisters hatching a plan to marry off their recently widowed brother, whom they call "the Professor."

17

Ringing the Bell
with One Foot in the Grave

Mehri Yalfani

Aqdas placed the tray of Persian tea glasses with their little saucers on the kitchen table. Akram stood next to the sink, water streaming over her hands onto the dishes.

"Put them here."

"No, these I'll wash. You're tired out."

"I'm not tired. Put them right here. Bring whatever else there is and I'll wash it. It's already getting dark out."

"You won't stay here tonight?"

"No, I've got to go. Haj Aqa and Mohsen are all alone. If I'm not there, they'll leave the house in the morning without any breakfast."

Aqdas set the tray of tea glasses next to her sister and left the kitchen. She brought back a few ashtrays, some full and some half-empty, along with a plate of half-eaten *halvâ*. The water streamed out of the faucet. Outside the window, it was now completely dark.

Akram looked over her shoulder at Aqdas and asked, "There's no more?"

"No." Aqdas emptied the ashtrays in the garbage.

"What are they doing?"

"Sitting there."

"Aren't they talking?"

"Not much. Abdollah doesn't quite speak the same way any-more. I don't know, have you noticed? Since he got here yester-day, he's hardly opened his mouth to say a word. I tried a few times to get him to talking. A couple times he said some things that didn't make any sense. He kept saying, 'Sorry.' What in the world does Sari have to do with Tehran![14] Do you suppose he's lost his bearings?"

Akram reached out to take the ashtrays. Casting a glance at the plate of *halva*, she said, "Put that back in the serving dish and give me the plate so I can wash it."

Aqdas took out the large bowl of *halva*, now half-empty, from the refrigerator and scraped the *halva* off the plate into a corner of the bowl. With her finger, she put a dollop of *halva* in her mouth. "This *halva* turned out marvellous. God rest her soul! She used to make a wonderful *halva*, herself."

She gave Akram the plate, sat down on a chair and stared out the window into the darkness. She took out a cigarette and lit it up. She drew the smoke into her lungs.

Akram turned around and looked at her. "Poor thing, she died so young. It wasn't time for her to go yet."

"She's gone and left us to deal with all the headache. How will the poor Professor manage, now?"

Akram put the last plate, still dripping with water, in the plas-tic dish rack next to the sink. She held the sponge under the water faucet and wrung it out in her hands. She wiped it over the rim of the sink and the edges of the counter and placed it back in the little dish at the side of the sink. Then she washed her hands under the faucet. Aqdas took a second puff on her cigarette, inhaling deeply. As she let it out, Akram turned off the water and dried her hands with a towel. She sat down on a chair and quickly lit a cigarette. "I was thinking about the Professor all afternoon. What about his

---

[14] Abdollah is saying the English word, "sorry," which Aqdas has mistaken for the similar sounding name of a town in northern Iran, Sâri, which is a good distance away from Tehran.

work? He can't manage without a wife. In this big house.....he's not even retired, at least then he'd be at home and could look after everything himself. After all, it's not much work to take care of just one person."

Aqdas shifted her gaze from the window to her sister. Aqdas had set down her cigarette on the ashtray and watched the thick smoke emerge from her sister's thin lips. "What do you mean it's not much work! A big house like this? And the Professor has to go to work in the morning and doesn't get home until evening. And even at home he's busy with work, as you can see. He has to correct his students' homework. Poor Masumeh! Don't you remember how she always had her hand to her heart?"

"She died so young! The poor thing was barely forty-eight."

"And to think of it! Remember how mother, God rest her soul, used to say that when they had gone to ask for Masumeh's hand in marriage, her family had complained that the groom is too old?!"

"Too old?! What nonsense. How old could he have been, anyway?"

"Thirty-five. But, then, Masumeh had not yet turned eighteen. Poor thing, life wore her out so soon."

"It was the cancer that made her old. In these last couple years she aged twenty years."

"Damn cancer! She should have lived much longer. She held her husband together."

"You see, sister dear! When I used to tell her she should have more kids, you all mocked me. She gave birth to two boys and then bolted the door."

"The Professor didn't want more kids. He told me so himself. But Masumeh, well, she wanted a girl. The last few weeks, when she was bedridden and couldn't even go to the bathroom, she kept saying that if she had a daughter, she wouldn't be forced to have a stranger take care of her. Once I helped sit her on a bedpan. Poor thing, how she sweated; it was embarrassing for her, after all."

Akram took a deep drag on her cigarette. "What are we going to do now? I've got to go. Anyway, what good is a daughter? I've got one of my own. She just up and left. I mean, she had to follow wherever her husband and kids went. You give birth to a daughter, she belongs to others. Give birth to a son, he belongs to others.

Children are just not faithful."

"Well, sis, as long as they are healthy. You shouldn't hope for anything more. If you send them abroad, you lose them too. Take Abdollah, here. How poor Masumeh had her hopes set on seeing her sons! And as for the other one, Mahmud never even came at all."

"He must have been unable to make it. These days travel is no joking matter."

"They say he's not amounted to much; as for this one, he's dazed and confused. Have you listened to him talk? He gets some words all mixed up and you can't understand him. I don't know what 'excuse' is supposed to mean."

"Listen, sis, I have to go." Akram looked at her watch. "But before I go, I have something to tell you; think it over. It occurred to me today, while Khadijeh was here. What do you think about having Khadijeh's daughter come here?"

"I don't understand what you mean."

"I mean Golnaz. Khadijeh's older daughter. Khadijeh, herself, wouldn't mind to place her daughter with a family she can trust. She is really good with sweeping, cleaning and washing. Not so bad looking, either." Akram paused momentarily, and a faint smile formed on her lips. She continued, "We'll quietly marry her to the Professor so their relationship won't be illicit."[15]

Aqdas looked dubiously at her sister and fell to thinking.

"What do you think?," asked Akram. "We cannot come here every day, make lunch and dinner for the Professor and look after a house as big as this. On the other hand, we cannot just abandon him and pray that everything turns out all right. What would people say? He's our brother, he's family. And, as you know, men just haven't got a clue. He hasn't dirtied his fingers even once in his life. He doesn't know how to take care of himself. He might do something to himself one day, like pour rat-poison in his food instead of salt by mistake. Then we'd have to answer to him and

---

[15] According to Iranian custom and religious law, a man and woman who are not related either by blood or marriage are not permitted to converse at length with one another or be alone in each other's company.

God for the rest of our lives."

Aqdas was lost in thought. After a while, she fixed a steady gaze on her sister and asked, "You mean Khadijeh would be willing to marry off Golnaz to the Professor?"

"Why wouldn't she? She should thank her lucky stars. The girl's missing a few marbles, you know. So far nobody has come asking for her. You know how maids and laundry women are—they marry off their daughters young. Khadijeh's second girl is already spoken for. Her uncle's boy has come to Tehran from the villages and is working in a factory. It looks as if they'll be married in the summer."

"Yes, sister, but be reasonable. How can you marry off a half-witted girl? Do you think the Professor would go for it?"

"I'll fix it, he'll agree. You don't know men. The Professor always had an eye for women. Don't you remember how Masumeh quarreled with him several times and went off to her father's house? All because of the Professor's fooling around."

"But with a servant girl?"

"Don't worry about it, I'll take care of all that. The thing is that I can't be coming here every day and night all by myself. You know what kind of a man Haj Aqa is—jealous and mean. He imagines I've got a secret rendezvous set up here. He can't bear to see me lift a finger even for my own brother and sister. You'd think I was his slave, body and soul. What can I do? I can't fight with him all my life, after all. Besides, as God and the Prophet have said, a woman must serve her husband. Well, a body's brother has a claim on her, too. I have to figure out some way to work this out, or people will talk. So, what do you think?"

"I just don't know. If you think it will work, well, go ahead and do it. First of all, you've got to get the Professor to go along with it. The Professor is no corner grocer, you know. He's been respected all his life, he teaches in the University. Boys and girls study under his direction. Now, how about if you tell him to get involved with one of his female students? Girls are always falling in love with their teachers. Why, I myself fell in love with my religious studies teacher when I was in the seventh grade."

"Mr. Fotuhi?"

"Yeah."

"You have lousy taste!"

"Well, I was just a kid, I didn't know any better."

"But you're lucky your husband is not like Mr. Fotuhi, or else...."

"Or else what? He was like Mr. Fotuhi. I just had to put up with him. There's no getting around it."

Akram got up. She looked out the window in the kitchen. The house light was on. "I'm going to go call Haj Aqa and have him come get me. There's no transportation at this time of night." When she came back, Aqdas had poured two glasses of tea and put them on the tray. "Who are those for?"

"For Abdollah and the Professor."

"Pour one for me, too."

Aqdas poured one tea, set it in front of her sister and went into the next room. When she came back Akram asked, "What were they doing?"

"The Professor is sitting at his desk leafing through a pile of papers and Abdollah was reading a book."

"Shall we go in the other room and sit with them for a while?"

"What for? They don't talk with us," said Aqdas. "Do you really think the plan will work?"

"What plan?"

"What you were saying just now—marrying Khadijeh's girl to the Professor."

"And why not? It's the only way."

"And if Golnaz should get pregnant, what then?"

Akram pondered the matter. She got up and poured herself another tea. She held the hot tea to her lips and took a sip. "Do you want tea?," she asked.

"No."

"I hadn't thought of that. We have to direct her to be careful."

"What do you mean, direct?! You can't follow her into the bed between the sheets! What if she feels like having kids? Once the Professor is her legal husband? She must want kids. Khadijeh probably wouldn't mind to have a grandchild by the Professor, either. In the end, some of his money and estate would go to her."

"I hadn't thought of that. No ringing the bell with a foot in the grave; no, she mustn't get pregnant."

"You'd have to fix it before the marriage. How would it be if we take her to a doctor and have her tubes tied?"

"How? You can't hand over a virgin girl to the midwife."

"So you see, it's not as easy as you think."

"We have to have a talk with the Professor. He must be made to understand to take precautions. The Professor is not terribly fond of kids. As you know, Masumeh only had two kids."

"And what if one day the girl gets pregnant by somebody else? After all, a seventeen or eighteen year-old girl is not going to be satisfied with a sixty-five year-old man. What if it happens she gets pregnant, huh? What's more, you say she's not got all her marbles. What would people say? Don't you think it will make things worse?"

"How should I know? Anyway, we have to think of something. Running the Professor's household is too big a job for you and me."

"It seems to me you have to plant the notion in the Professor's head for him to go and find a girl for himself. One of his students. If they work something out on their own, there'd be no headache for us to deal with."

"Nonsense, sis. An educated girl would never marry a sixty-five year-old man."

"Who says she wouldn't? Haven't you heard about Dr. Farhudi? He's just about the same age as our Professor? He's taken a twenty year-old girl to wife."

"Really? When?"

"Haven't you heard? His first wife isn't speaking to him and has gotten up and left."

"Mahin Khanum? With four kids?"

"Yeah. The kids are all grown. It seems the Doctor falls in love with one of his patients, or one of his patients with him. I don't know....And then he secretly takes her as a *sigheh*. Then it happens that the girl gets pregnant. She must be about to deliver any day now. The Doctor has legally married her."

"Where did you hear all this?"

"I heard it just today. It's becoming a real scandal. Parvin Khanum was telling me about it."

"The poor woman. What will she do now?"

"I told you, she's stopped speaking to him and has gone to her family in Mashhad. I think she wants to get a divorce."

Akram got up and went to the window. "I don't know what's keeping him. You can't leave these damn men alone for even one night. Right away they start chasing after women."

Aqdas laughed and said, "You're the one who's going back to the side of your husband. You'll go and leave me here all alone."

"You, your husband is not a raffish bastard."

"How would you know? As the saying goes, `Have no fear of men who bark and riot; beware the one who acts all calm and quiet.'"

The sound of a car's brakes made her get up. "He's here; I'm going. You go talk to the Professor. Get him to go along with the plan."

"Have you thought the thing through to the end?"

"We'll think about that later."

"But, sister, at least wait until the poor woman is cold in her grave."

"Why worry about the poor woman's corpse? You have to think about the living."

Faribâ Vafi is from Tabriz in the northwest of Iran, where she was born in 1962. She is a housewife and has two children. Her first story, "*You're at Peace Now, Father*" (*Râhat shodi pedar*), was published in 1988 in the journal *Âdineh*. Several of her stories have been published in various literary journals in Iran, and in collections of short stories by contemporary Iranian writers. She has prepared a collection of her stories called *At the Back of the Stage* (*Dar `omq-e sahneh*), which will soon be published. The story presented here is part of a trilogy of stories tracing the experience of several characters in an Iranian prison, including the story "*Read to Me*" ("*Barâm be-khvun*") published in the journal *Shetâb* in 1993. The controversial topic of these stories has made it difficult for Ms. Vafi to find publishers in Iran willing to assume the possible consequences of publication.

The story presented here, "*The Flight of the Sun*" ("*Farâr-e âftâb*," published in *Simorgh*, no. 52, Mission Viejo, CA, September 1994 pp. 28-29), depicts the pangs of conscience of a guard in a woman's prison in contemporary Iran when she is ordered to lash one of the inmates.

18

The Flight of the Sun

Fariba Vafi

It was the first time, after working there for three months, that Mrs. Amini was whipping a convict. The inmates had wrapped themselves in their chadors and were sitting around the courtyard, getting ready to watch the show. There was a blanket spread out in the middle of the courtyard and an inmate, with her big fat body, was lying flat on it, gasping for breath. Tahereh's kid was screaming, and Madam Qiyasi was yelling at Tahereh, "Shut him up! The little bastard..."

Until Mrs. Amini felt the wooden handle of the whip, she imagined that she could get out of doing the deed if she wanted to. But she had been unable to avoid it and now, in disbelief, she stared at the whip in her hand and felt that she no longer knew who she was.

The prison guard was impatient: "Ma'am, carry out the sentence!"

It was a few hours before noon. It was hot and Mrs. Amini's hands had broken out in a sweat. She took a few steps forward and looked at the inmate. Madam Qiyasi said, "Do it, Ma'am."

Mrs. Amini raised the whip and brought down the first blow. The whip made a dull crack in her ears. When she struck the second blow, the color had left her cheeks and her knees trembled visibly. Before she finished striking the third blow, Madam Qiyasi rushed towards her, snatched the whip roughly from her hands and, frothing at the mouth, said, "Ma'am, the way you are whipping, the prisoner's underwear won't even flinch."

She raised the whip, snapped it in the air and struck the next blow. This time the whip cracked sharply. The lashes rained down one after another. The inmate groaned, "Awwwh!...." Madam Qiyasi gave her a fierce kick in the side: "Spare me your Awwwhs."

The inmate's groaning stopped. Madam Qiyasi whipped her harder. Mrs. Amini did not stay until all the lashes were inflicted. She came back to the office and drank a glass of water, but did not feel any better. She squeezed her throat with her fingers. Madam Qiyasi came into the office. Her face was sweaty. She looked at Mrs. Amini contemptuously.

"You're fresh out of school. You think one shouldn't do such things. You still have a lot to learn about this crowd. You have to beat these animals. I've been working here for fifteen years and I know these people better than they know themselves. These are wanton women who stuff their mouths with a big wad of chewing gum, a morsel of bread and some vegetables... They barely even notice it when they're whipped....They leave the prison, go about their illegal activities and return again to prison. You just have to get used to it. Jail is no place to let your guard down. If you turn your head for an instant, they'll pull a fast one on you."

The rough manly voice of Madam Qiyasi was giving her a headache. She looked at her; her eyes seemed to be dimmer and the infected pimples on her face appeared to have broken open. She wanted to avoid seeing her mouth and the oozing white froth around its corners, but every time she looked at her mouth, she swallowed her saliva. She wanted to get out. She felt that she could no longer breathe. Suddenly, she exhaled: "It's too hot..."

Madam Qiyasi looked at her, annoyed: "Next time, you'll do the whipping. Got it?"

The next time came very soon. Maryam was to be released but had forty lashes coming to her. Mrs. Amini was coming from guard duty and stood behind the ward, not wanting to come in. The cats were wriggling through the garbage behind the prison ward, and the air was filled with the peculiar heavy odor of the prison.

A male inmate was sitting in the shade, weaving a belt and murmuring to himself under his breath. Mrs. Amini sat down, staring at the high wall of the prison. She tried to imagine the other side of the wall. She knew that they had recently planted flowers in the square on the other side of the wall—what kind of flowers were they? "I'll go there tomorrow and see," she thought, but the thought did not make her happy at all. The prison director's words echoed in her ear: "A jail keeper himself is a prisoner—a prisoner with responsibility."

The voices of the female inmates could be heard from the prison courtyard. She did not want to move. "Maryam must have been brought back from the prison doctor's office by now. I wish the doctor had said that Maryam could not endure a whipping. I've got to go in."

But she did not budge. She felt tired. She wanted to think about something nice, something outside the prison walls. It was almost evening—the sunlight was creeping along the prison wall. The fact that she had been assigned to whip Maryam gave her no peace. She remembered the first day when the guard brought Maryam to the ward. The inmates had gathered around her. Afaq the Junkie contemptuously said, "I bet she had an illicit affair..."

Robab the Procuress swung her heavy frame in front of Maryam and wiped the saliva off her chops: "Yes, it must have been. She's quite a dish...."

Sorayya, a long-term inmate of the ward, winked at her and softly said, "How many men did you do it with, dear?"

Maryam just stared ahead dumbfounded. All of a sudden she hid her terrified face in her worn chador and began crying like a baby.

Mrs. Amini sat there in silent dejection. Madam Qiyasi was watching her out of the corner of her eye and yelling at the inmates who had gathered behind the glass door of the office. When the prison official came in, accompanied by an assistant holding the whip and the punishment report form, Maryam hurried forward and lay down on the blanket spread out in the middle of the courtyard. Madam Qiyasi shot after her like lightning, grabbed her arm and made her get up.

"Hold on just a minute... What's all this you're wearing?"

Maryam lost her wits and began to stutter.... Mrs. Amini took her face in both hands and bit her lip. Her cheeks were burning. Madam Qiyasi triumphantly dragged Maryam to the office, like someone who had just made an important discovery, and said in a loud voice dripping with sarcasm: "Well, well, well! Who's taught you to wear all these clothes in this heat?"

Maryam was crying: "Ma'am, I'm guilty."

Madam Qiyasi fell upon Maryam, punching and kicking her. Everyone was glued to their spots by Maryam's earsplitting cries.

"You're guilty...and you're full of shit."

Maryam took off all of her clothes. Mrs. Amini was standing in the corner, feeling cold.

Madam Qiyasi said, "Get down on all fours!" She grabbed the whip from the prison employee's hand and gave it to Mrs. Amini. "Whip her like a jail keeper, Ma'am. If you spoil these inmates, they'll fill the whole world up with little bastards."

The inmates were standing behind the glass door of the office, straining their necks out of curiosity and whispering to one another. The prison guard was standing outside; the prison employee, while quieting the inmates, was staring at Maryam's delicate body, all crumpled up and quivering in her chador. Mrs. Amini closed her eyes and struck her. Madam Qiyasi piped up: "Whip her harder."

Mrs. Amini swung harder. The voices of the inmates, who had begun rhythmically counting out the blows, made the image of a long deserted tunnel appear before her eyes. She was moving forward in this dark corridor and, in a state of nervous agitation, whipping the inmate. For an instant the brightness outside the tunnel struck her eyes and she saw the sun entangled in the barbed wires surrounding the prison. It was as if the sun was trying to escape.

Maryam wailed: "It's killing me, sister...Awwwwh!...it's killing me."

Mrs. Amini was whipping her. The swift, rhythmic back-and-forth movement of the whip had made her giddy. Her head swam with sounds.

A voice said, "It's done!"

Her fingers numb, she gave the whip back to the prison employee and signed the report. She went out of the office. She stood at the top of the stairs of the yard and looked around like someone unfamiliar with the place. She was dizzy. She immediately went back to the office, took her purse down from the closet and left the ward, paying no attention to Madam Qiyasi's threatening inquiries and the amazed stares of the inmates. When she made it beyond the prison walls, she saw the sun, freed from the barbed wires, drowning the newly-planted flowers of the square in light.

Glossary

Abâ: A loose, wide-sleeved robe, worn as an outer garment by traditional Iranian men.

Berenji: Cookies made with rice flour, butter and poppy seeds that melt in your mouth.

Behesht-e Zahrâ Cemetery: The largest Muslim cemetery in Tehran.

Chehel Sotun: Chehel Sotun (The Forty Columns) was built in Isfahan by Shah Abbas I of the Safavid dynasty. It was a throne room used chiefly for the reception of distinguished visitors and ambassadors, but is now a tourist site.

Damâvand: A town and district near Mt. Damavand, an extinct volcano north of Tehran, the highest peak in the Alborz range, which defines the horizon north of Tehran.

Fâludeh: A cool fruit slush beverage with sweet noodles. "Traditional" Iranian ice cream is usually flavored with rose-water and has nuggets of cream and pistachios in it.

Fesenjân: A traditional Iranian casserole dish of chicken cooked in a sauce of ground walnuts and pomegranate syrup, served over a bed of rice. It is a fairly labor-intensive dish to prepare.

Hâfezieh: The tomb of Hafez, Iran's most popular poet. Hafez died in 1390. He was buried in the garden of Mossalla in Shiraz, which in his honor is now called Hafezieh.

Halvâ: A sweet paste of sugar, flour, oil and saffron, eaten as a desert. Arabs and Turks also make halvâ, but with crushed sesame seeds.

Hezbullâh: Literally "the Party of God," is a loosely organized vigilante band of conservative Shiite Musilms, drawn mostly from the urban poor, who played an important role, along with Komiteh and Revolutionary Guards, in enforcing - often by violent means - conservative Islamic policy. They also supplied many front-line soldiers for the war with Iraq and helped train and finance the Hezbullahis in Lebanon.

Karbalâ: A shrine city in Iraq, sacred for Shiites, to which pilgrimage is made. It is the place where Imam Husayn was killed by the forces of the Caliph Yazid in 680 A.D.

Komiteh (Revolutionary committees): Begun as defense bands protecting neighborhoods from anti-revolutionary activists, they were eventually taken over by Khomeini, purged of anti- or non-Islamic elements and put under central government authority. As a para-military arm, they were fundamental in suppressing leftist groups and others opposed to clerical rule and were greatly feared. In 1984, the energies of the Komiteh were directed to stopping drug-trafficking and making sure women observed the veil in public. In 1991, the Komitehs were absorbed into the regular police forces.

Korsi: A low wood frame holding a kerosene burner over which are draped quilts and blankets. Iranians used to sit around the korsi under the blankets to keep warm in winter.

Martyrs' Foundation: A foundation established after the outbreak of the Iran-Iraq War (1980-1988) to help the relatives of soldiers and volunteers killed in the fighting.

Nâser al-Din Shâh: A king of the Qajar dynasty who ruled Iran from 1848 until his assasination in 1896.

Shirin: Heroine of a verse romance, Khosrow and Shirin, by the

Persian poet Nezami of Ganjeh (ca. 1141-1203). Shirin (the name means "sweet"), a princess of Armenia, falls in love with a portrait of Khosrow, prince of Iran, and sets off to find him. On the 14th day of her journey, she stops to bathe in a wayside spring, and Khosrow, who has fortuitously arrived at the same spot, covertly spies her and is enamored - an episode popular with miniature painters.

Farhad, a sculptor, also falls in love with Shirin. Khosrow challenges him to cut a channel through Mount Bisutun in order to win Shirin and when Farhad has all but finished this super human task, Khosrow deceitfully sends a messenger with false news of Shirin's death. Farhad leaps from the rocks to his death. Khosrow's life is ended by an assassin's dagger as he sleeps beside Shirin; after preparing the body for burial, Shirin takes out the dagger and kills herself.

Sigheh: A temporary wife, who, according to Shi`ite law, can be married for a period of time specified beforehand by contract. Any children issuing from such a marriage are the financial responsibility of the husband. Under the Constitution of the Islamic Republic, a man may have four permanent wives and an indefinite number of temporary wives, if he is able to support them all.

Tâftun: A kind of Persian bread baked on heated pebbles in a furnace.

Târ: A traditional Persian instrument, a lute that more or less resembles the guitar (which is etymologically related). It is played by a plectrum.

About the Translators

Franklin Lewis is Mellon Lecturer in Persian at the University of Chicago. He holds a Ph.D. in Persian literature from the University of Chicago and his dissertation on the 12th-century mystical poet, Sana'i of Ghazna, received the Foundation for Iranian Studies' best dissertation award in 1995. He has published scholarly articles about the history of Persian literature as well as a number of translations of short stories and poems by such contemporary Iranian writers as Simin Daneshvar, Hushang Golshiri, Goli Taraqqi, Mahdokht-e Kashkuli and Ahmad Shamlu. He lives near Chicago with his wife and two daughters.

Farzin Yazdanfar holds Master's degrees from the University of Michigan in applied economics and Near Eastern Studies. He has contributed translations to *Stories From Iran: A Chicago Anthology 1921-1991*, and is a contributing writer to the journals *Rackham Journal of the Arts and Humanities, the Chicago Review*, and the Persian journals *Kelk, Simorgh, Daftar-e Hunar, Iran Nameh* and *Iranshenasi*. He has compiled and co-edited an anthology, which is a collection of short stories written by Iranian women between the years 1945 and 1989, entitled *"A Walnut sapling on Masih's Grave and Other Stories by Iranian Women."* He lives in Chicago.